Winter Kisses

3:AM Kisses Book 2

A Novella

D1526539

ADDISON MOORE

Edited by: Sarah Freese
Cover design by: Gaffey Media

Books by Addison Moore:

Elysian (Celestra Series Book 8)
Ephemeral (The Countenance Trilogy 1)
Evanescent (The Countenance Trilogy 2)
Entropy (The Countenance Trilogy 3)
Ethereal Knights (Celestra Knights)

Prologue

Laney

I used to believe in love. I used to believe that two people and one lifetime equaled happily ever after. I used to believe that the strong arms that once held me tight would always protect, never leave, never give up on us.

Maybe he didn't give up on us. Maybe I did.

At the end of the day, maybe we both did.

And yet, here I am in his penthouse, devoid of clothes, low on dignity, loaded with whiskey.

"Let me into your heart, Laney," he pleads with those deep navy eyes as we stand just shy of his bed. "Let me crush every memory you have of the two of us and make something new, something better, something that never disappoints because it doesn't know how." He dots a series of hot kisses slowly up my neck, and a shiver runs through me.

My skin touches his, and then it's over. I'm all in. Every last inch of me has been so thirsty for Ryder, and now, here I am, ready to drown in the cool spring of his affection while my entire body reanimates under his willful supervision. A part of me died last winter in a very real way, and, here he is, reawakening me, breathing life back into my soul by way of his mouth, his fingers—his bare flesh.

He pulls back and rakes over me with his slow gaze.

"Get in my bed," he growls it out, sharp like an order.

"If you want me in your bed you'll have to damn well put me there yourself."

Ryder gives the ghost of a smile.

And he does.

1

Can't Buy Me Love

Laney

Playing the part of a wench isn't easy, especially when the very people who have accused me of being the real deal are sitting in the front row. I'm sure that in just a few short minutes they'll be smirking at the way my boobs keep threatening to unleash themselves from this demonically tight corset.

"Good luck, Laney!" Baya helps adjust the seventeenth-century ball gown I've crammed myself into.

"Don't say that!" Roxy swats Baya as she pushes me onto the stage with the rest of the cast. "Break a leg!"

I scuttle out, trying not to focus on the fact I spotted my ex in the crowd just a few minutes ago, and now I'm nervous as hell, and breaking a leg seems a literal possibility in my sky-high heels.

It's the night of the *Gala of the Stars*, an annual fundraiser for the drama department, but if I had known who would be here, gawking at both me and my cleavage, I would have gladly bowed out. Of course, the trauma of the evening is multiplied a thousand times over, due to the fact my ex-boyfriend happens to be sitting front and center, smack in between his judgmental mother and the girl he left me for. Well, I'm not sure if he really left me for Meg, but, nevertheless, they're an arms length apart.

I move along with the rest of the drama department as we walk the expanse of the stage like runway models. Tonight we'll be auctioned off like objects to the highest bidder in the name of school spirit—and, hopefully for the department, some serious cold hard cash.

I take the turn at the head of the stage and force my eyes to remain on the girl in front of me. I lose myself in the bird's nest her hair has been teased into, the full crimson gown she's wearing that balloons from her waist like a parachute.

Walk the line, I keep telling myself. Madame Thenardier doesn't need to smile, and neither do I.

A pressing heat fills me as I pass my ex. The air crackles, it sizzles and snaps from his direction. Ryder Capwell commands the attention of every estrogen bearing female in the room—and, damn straight, he gets it.

Finally the long tongue of the stage is behind me as I scurry back to the curtain and peer out at the crowd. I see my mother and sister, Izzy, as they wave to me from the side. Even though Izzy is five years older, we still look like twins with the long dark hair, the stonewashed blue eyes.

Mom strums her fingers over the table, a clear sign she's anxious about something. I'm guessing she's seen the Capwells and is ready to bolt like a cat from a bathtub. Her jet-black hair curls out of her head like claws, and she insists on wearing the brightest shade of pink lipstick known to man. Despite the fact Mom is a larger woman, no matter what her size, her lips are the first and last thing you see when she's coming and going. She's tough as nails but independent and fierce to a fault. I've always admired those attributes about her most. Everybody respects my mother, well except for Rue Capwell. According to Rue, my mother is the kind of slimy invertebrate you find living under the belly of a rock.

Mom points a finger at Ryder and shakes her head at me. She isn't exactly Ryder's biggest fan, then again, neither am I. But no matter how hard I try, my eyes gravitate to him like fire to oxygen. This is the kind of compulsory mess that no matter how much effort you put into avoiding, you know what the outcome will be. Ryder Capwell still has a very real piece of me. I'm going down in flames, I can feel it, and I'm already enjoying the burn.

I cast my eyes over his perfect eminence for just a moment. All I can see from this vantage point is his blessed-by-God face—that perfect bone structure, his Roman nose. The muscles in his jaw pop as he darts a look this way, and I'm quick to jump back from his line of vision. For just a brief moment he was examining me in the way that only his gorgeous eyes could do. Ryder had a way of bringing me to life like a picture slowly developing before his beautiful eyes. He brought out the color in me— the vibrancy from deep within my soul that I never knew existed.

"Holy hell," I mutter, diving back behind the curtain as my best friends Baya and Roxy try to discourage me from hanging myself from the rafters. Honestly, a public hanging seems a much more appealing option than facing Ryder, especially since Meg boyfriend-fucking Collins has planted herself right next to him. Well, I seriously doubt she's fucked him outside of her wildest dreams, at least I hope not, but, that too, seems beside the point because my blood boils at the sight of her, and the urge to puke is coming on strong. Maybe I should go with it. Who knows? A little projectile vomiting might be exactly what the psychiatrist ordered, that is if I land my target. Either Meg or Ryder's mother will do. Ryder doesn't deserve my vomit.

"Every person on the planet who hates me is here tonight—and, by the way"—I look to Roxy—"I'm including my own mother in that equation." Quite possibly my sister, but that's probably not true—Izzy and I just aren't that close.

"My mother doesn't hate you." Roxy averts her eyes as if this were an impossibility.

Baya touches her hand to her chest while her dark hair quivers back. "And I'm sure *your* mother doesn't hate you." Baya is gorgeous, and she's got a body for miles. It's no wonder my friend Bryson fell so hard for her. I'm glad they're happy—hell, I'm glad someone's happy.

"Oh, you don't know my mother," I'm quick to correct. "And, for the record"—I turn to Roxy—"you don't know *your* mother either. Hate is just the tip of the iceberg of what that woman feels for me." I look to Baya. "True story. She hates me and loves Meg Collins." Meg comes from money, was gently reared, and annoyingly insisted on calling my ex-boyfriend's mother, *mom,* long before we were ever over. "Face it, Rox, both your mother and Meg are thrilled that Ryder and I called it quits."

"Ryder didn't call anything quits—you did." Roxy tugs at my corset until my boobs pop up, creating a dramatic décolleté that Ryder only wishes he could bury his face in. The dress I'm wearing has the girls on a perch, ready and willing to jump off the ledge at a moment's notice. The gown in general is a period piece, a dirty blue brocade with a full bell skirt and tight waist, low cut to the nipple line, and I must say I look every part the wench. Actually I'm Madame Thenardier the keeper of the inn. Whitney Briggs is putting on *Les Mis* for their Winter Spectacular, so here we are at the country club trying to raise funds for the department.

"I don't care who called it quits. The important thing is that it's over." I untie my bustle only to retie it six times tighter than before. "To hell with breathing, I have far more important things to do like bring you-know-who to his drop-dead gorgeous knees for everything he put me through last year."

"Hey, relax. Nobody is out to get you," Baya says it sweetly while combing the hair away from my face. "Can I ask what happened with you and—" She ticks her head toward the crowd. I have a very strict do-not-use-the-asshole's-name-in-my-presence rule, and if you should feel the need, kindly replace his moniker with Bastard, or what he's more formally known as, Rat Bastard.

"Nothing happened." Roxy dares defy the circumstances that got the breakup ball rolling, thus openly rejecting my reasoning for the horrible relationship demise. "My brother still loves her." Roxy's eyes swell with tears. "Laney is just too stubborn to hear the truth. See this, Baya? This is what happens when someone isn't willing to listen to a logical explanation. She just hopped to her own conclusions and, poof, a thing of beauty disappeared into thin air."

"I'm not listening." I pick up my dress and stalk off toward Bing Chase, my partner in *Les Mis* crime who happens to play the part of my perverted husband.

"You need a hit?" He holds out a bottle of Seagram's 7, and I'm quick to snatch it from him. I put my lips to the tip and effectively pour the brown brew down my throat, easy as drinking fire.

"Slow down, girl." He tries to muscle it away from me, but I continue to chug until my insides threaten to detonate like a nuclear warhead.

The choir finishes up a sassy version of *Jingle Bells,* and the master of ceremonies takes his place at the podium once again.

"Ladies and gentlemen of this fine establishment," he rambles it out with all of the theatrics of a circus conductor. "Whitney Briggs dramatic arts and dance department is proud to present a snippet of the Winter Spectacular's prized presentation, *Les Miserables*. Feast your eyes on the fine cast as ten title characters are auctioned off as a part of our evening with the stars. Open your wallets and your hearts. All proceeds go directly to the department. And, now, please put your hands together as we present, *Master of the House*."

The crowd breaks out into a mild applause, and I refuse to pan the front row. I refuse to let Ryder Capwell catch me glancing in his direction—for him to see even one hint of desperation in my eyes. God forbid I lock eyes with Meg or his mother for that matter—my ultra-pointy stilettos might go flying. And believe you me these are some serious weapons of mass destruction, or at least worthy of a good stabbing. They're the killing-cockroaches-in-the-corner variety, but they're cute as hell, never mind the fact they're cutting off the circulation to my pinky toes. I swear the girl in the costume department hates me. This isn't the first time she's cursed me with something that's capable of a quasi-maiming.

Bing plucks the bottle from my hands. "We're on, kid." The music starts up, and we saunter out with the ensemble. I try to keep my focus on Bing while he wails away his solo, but my thighs are shaking just being this close to Ryder. It's like I can sense him in the room. My chest heaves for no good reason, my skin gets hot then cold, then sticky and clammy because, truth be told, that man still has a very real physical effect on me—also there was whiskey.

Nevertheless Ryder Capwell is a god, fit for altar worship and eternal veneration all of which I was physically and mentally prepared to do until he left me alone and naked in bed one night. He hightailed it back to his mother's house to once again rescue the forever damsel in distress, Maniacal Meg.

Anyway, he apologized until his balls were blue in the face and asked what he could do to make it better— that he would do absolutely anything, so I asked the only logical thing I could think of. I told him to stay the hell away from me. I meant it at the time, but damn it all to hell if I haven't hated myself just a little this past year for invoking such a harsh punishment. And, Ryder being the moral upstanding, albeit Rat Bastard, kind of a guy he is, upheld his end of the Laney embargo, and we haven't been face-to-face in twelve solid months. I mean, he tried, but I was quick to instate Newton's third law of *e*-motion: for every one of his actions, I enlisted an opposite and equal *reaction*—ready and willing to deflect his efforts. For instance—he called, I ignored. He texted, I blocked. He emailed, I unopened.

The tragedy of it all is that I used to believe in love. I used believe in Ryder and me. I thought we would last. I thought we had forever in our grasp, but we were just a lie. He couldn't hold me up over the other women in his life. Instead, I was sloshing around the bottom somewhere beneath his mother and Meg, both of whom took turns urinating on me.

Bing stomps over and gives a stern look. It's only then I realize the music is recuing itself on a loop as the band patiently waits for me to jump into the number.

"Crap," I hiss, scuttling further onto the stage, and the audience chortles along with the cast—although the cast chortling happens to be scripted.

I belt out my number, slow, seductive, and I don't squirm like I usually do during rehearsals when Bing pushes Guy Richards' face between my boobs. This time I sort of jump into him, increasing his plunge into my cleavage, and I can actually feel him breathing right over my skin. I bend my neck back and let out a breathy sigh as if I'm enjoying the shit out of it because secretly I want Ryder to die a thousand slow deaths knowing his face will never again venture to be where Guy Richards' lucky nostrils have landed.

I make the mistake of glancing down at his mother— *Rue*. There she is with her freshly died auburn hair, the veins in her neck distending as she forces a smile on those dry orange lips.

Last winter, Ryder's mother called me a common street whore. Yes, she went there. The insult came after I sent him a private picture of me changing for a play that I was starring in, *Annie*. I thought it was hilarious the way I looked with my cupie-doll makeup and curly red wig with nothing else on but my pink lace bra and matching thong, so I took a selfie and shot him one. Only Ryder was at his parent's house, and his mother somehow got ahold of my need for redheaded self-expression of the Victoria Secret variety, and, well, the word *whore* bubbled from her lips. Of course, Ryder didn't relay the message, Meg did, but when I had the big confrontation last Christmas Eve, Ruthless Rue, a.k.a. the woman I myself shall never call "mom," didn't bother to deny it. Instead she backed it up with a potshot at my own mother that went something like, *the apple doesn't fall far from the tree.*

Anyway, Rue Capwell is the cruelest most judgmental person on the planet, and I have no problem saying that, considering she's my best friend's mother because it just so happens to be a solid fact. To deny it would be akin to saying that the earth is flat, or that a shoe sale at Macy's is a thing to be ignored.

Meg is no angel either. When I think of the night it all came crashing down for Ryder and me, it's her naked body that burns into my mind. I'd rather stick my face in a hot skillet than relive any part of it. There are a lot of words to describe a person like Meg, and they're all way too nice for her—a canine of a certain gender, a delicate part of the female anatomy. But I'm not going there. I couldn't hate her more if I tried.

In the end, his mother and Meg wore me down. I would never be enough for his mother, and Meg would never quit. The saddest part of the equation was that Ryder never seemed to believe me when it came to his mother's special brand of cruelty. He was always ready with an excuse, too quick to overlook her grievances. His mother and Meg created an ocean of hurt, and time after time Ryder set me down in it, surrendering me to the wind like a cheap paper boat.

I finish up the solo portion of my number, and the ensemble joins in as we round out the scene together. God—I hate when my attention is spliced in two while I'm trying to perform. It's a serious mindfuck because on one hand I'm flaunting my cleavage trying to convey this clever dialogue through song while I'm really off somewhere in my brain having hot make-up sex and simultaneously strangling my ex.

Then, without warning, my eyes commit the biggest grievance of all. I glance down, and the unthinkable happens—our eyes lock, and I freeze solid.

Ryder Capwell still very much has me in more ways than one, whether I like it or not.

His ebony-colored hair is combed back in lustrous waves, a little longer than it was last year. His navy eyes sear right through to my soul while my panties spontaneously combust beneath my tattered gown. Swear to God, smoke is going to plume from under my skirt at any moment, and there aren't enough fire extinguishers in the world to douse these flames. My nipples inch out of my costume and ache to look at him themselves while my stomach ignites in a ball of fire just imagining the things he can do to me with those oversized hands, that long, serpentine tongue, his soft-as-air lips. Ryder looks impeccable tonight in his inky black suit, his silver tie—luscious enough to bind my wrists with. Every part of me screams for him to touch me, and all the while our gaze is immovable as concrete.

Crap.

I've broken my sacred rule, and now, here I am, openly lusting for the entire world to see—his mother—Meg.

Damn it all to hell.

Ryder Capwell still very much holds my heart.

Ryder

She's looking at me.

Holy shit if Laney Sawyer didn't just land those sweet sky blue eyes right over my person, twice in one evening. I take her in with those sugared lips, that black hair that makes her eyes glow like a pair of swimming pools.

The trace of a smile plays on my lips, but I won't give it.

The audience breaks into applause as the performance comes to a close, but I don't move or breathe or think one lewd thought of her in that carnal catastrophe of a costume. Instead, for one fleeting moment, I pretend we're still Laney and Ryder, and that later I'll be mapping out every inch of her lily-white skin with my mouth. An image of her beneath me with her dress hiked above her hips takes over, and there goes the ridiculous idea of not thinking one lewd thought about her tonight.

The truth is, I've had nothing but a stream of insanely indecent thoughts about Laney for the past twelve months. It's been one long porn flick starring the two of us, and just when I think they can't get any lewder or cruder, I surprise the hell out of myself. There have been clowns, and monkeys, and, hell, I've even thrown in a bottle of crazy glue a time or two because without Laney around to keep me reasonably sane I tend to go off the rails a little both in and out of my fucked up imagination.

I can't help it. I gave her my heart—buried it deep inside her, and I never want it back. There's no one out there for me but Laney Sawyer, and I couldn't care less if I was making a scene or much to mother's embarrassment, a fool of myself by holding Laney's beautiful eyes hostage with mine.

To hell with the world, I'm about half a second away from getting down on my knees and begging her to take me back.

The MC claps his way to the mike, and it sputters and pops as his hands get too close to the receiver. He waves over at the cast, and that's when Laney takes a bow and the spell is forcibly broken—our magic moment gone too soon, just as swift and unexpected as our relationship was revoked.

My eyes land on the numbered paddles on the table because I know what's coming next. All night I've watched as my mother and her socialite cohorts have bid on item after item to help raise funds for the drama department, and now, the unthinkable is about to go down. Laney, herself, is about to be put on the block in the name of Whitney Briggs.

The MC barters away half the cast before he finally gets to beautiful, sweet Laney, and my gut cinches as she parades around the stage in full character. She's sassing it up to a room full of catcalls, mostly from the *Les Mis* ensemble, but, still, she'll always be my girl, and deep down I can't stand the thought of anyone else touching her, let alone ogling her body for retail purposes.

Laney pauses with her back to me, sending a clear message that this is one business opportunity both me and my dick are welcome to sit out. Laney would rather cover herself with honey and roll in a pile of fire ants than have anything to do with my dick or my dollars.

The auction starts, and, much to my relief, the only people bidding for Laney's company are a handful of women. A boulder rolls right off my chest because for a second there I envisioned some preppy prince charming riding in and sweeping her away to his frat house. With my luck they'd fall in love, and Laney would get right to the task of having an entire herd of preppy babies. But I won't put up a fight if a few older women want to listen to her belt out a couple tunes for kicks. They can do brunch and call it a day. The university gets paid, and there's no harm no foul to Laney or her girl parts. Speaking of which, two of my favorite parts have been quivering for my attention ever since she stepped on stage.

Master of the House, I glare over at Guy Richards and withhold the urge to punch him in the neck. I've got a master of the house that wouldn't mind some of Laney's attention and a couple of innkeepers that could use some comfort themselves. It was all I could do to keep from clocking him after he did a face-plant in my girlfriend's chest. Not that she's my girlfriend anymore, or even a friend for that matter.

"Who else is up for a dining experience with this fine wench?" The MC points out at the crowd at random. "Dinner and a dance? One magic-filled night? Have her your way, hold the lettuce, pickles, cheese." A dull laugh circles the room at his lame attempt to make Laney sound like a cheap piece of meat.

Laney glances over her shoulder. She's biting down on her bottom lip, and my dick perks to attention ready to pick up the damn paddle itself.

"Right here," a male voice booms from the back. I turn to find Holt Edwards flashing his million-watt smile, and my jaw tightens. The last person Laney needs to be paired with is that loser. His brother and I are pretty close, but Holt took Laney out a few times after she dumped me with all of the emotional fanfare that the shit parade calls for. And now I can't stand the sight of him. I work with his brother, Bryson. Actually he's doing an internship at my father's company. The Edwards family own a bunch of bars, and one of them happens to be where Laney is currently employed. Holt and Bryson are twins—fraternal, but nonetheless, they look like one and the same, and for a while it was hard to sit in a meeting with Bryson because as much as it made no sense, I was constantly a little ticked at him.

My mother picks up her paddle and outbids the douche, and now I'm very fucking alarmed because I know for a fact Laney can't stand the sight of the woman who gave birth to me.

I give Mom that what-in-the-hell look, but she dismisses me with nothing more than a placid smile.

"Isn't this exciting?" Meg leans over in an effort to distract me. I shake my head for a moment, but it has nothing to do with whatever the hell she's going on about. Last year she worked in perfect synergy with my mother to wear Laney down, and I let it happen. Laney cried out to me from the quick sand, time and time again, and I waited until she was up to her eyebrows to notice. But it was too late.

Meg comes in close with her single strand of pearls wagging in my line of vision, but I never take my attention from Laney. If I had only done so right from the beginning, we wouldn't be in this predicament with me withholding my wallet, and, her, doing her best to avoid me in a tragically overcrowded world that's far too lonely for us to ever be apart. Laney moves toward center stage, her shoulder still strategically hiked in my direction.

Meg drones on and on about the weather, the over-decorated Christmas tree, the lights strung out over the ceiling, swaying like drunken stars, but I don't lose focus on what's really going on.

Holt outbids my mother, and the auctioneer rattles off, "Going once, going twice—"

I flip my paddle in the air without putting too much thought into it.

"Sold to the young man in the front. Hells bells and Jezebel! Pay the man, and take your new bride for a ride."

He moves on to the next cast member, and I sit there like an ass, panting out of breath because I just broke the last promise I ever made to her—the one to stay the hell away.

A guy from the drama department comes by with the bill, and I hand him my platinum card as if I were anteing up the tab at a restaurant.

Mom shifts in her seat as if she was sitting on a bed of tacks, as does Meg, and now there's a shitload of silence in our midst because I've just managed to stun them both to hell, myself included.

"Thank you, sir," says the guy dressed as a court jester, or an elf, or whatever caped crusader his tights are representing today. I take a breath and cut a quick glance over to my mother as he takes off with three thousand dollars of my hard-earned money.

My parents are of the school of thought that it's entirely up to their offspring to generate their own brand of wealth, and, lucky for me, because I've managed to do just that, thanks to some smart moves in the market. And now that I'm working for my father's advertising division, I'm amassing quite a nice nest egg at record pace. He's fine with me as a grunt worker, so long as I don't own the place one day.

Music filters in through the speakers, and the lights dim as couples migrate over to the dance floor.

Mom leans in. "It's always a nice philanthropic effort to make a donation." Her eyes swirl like pinwheels. "Don't feel like you need to take it any further. Half the people that bid will only take it so far. It's the thought that counts." She gives a little wink, but I can see the budding agitation that's making her sway. I used to think it was the farthest thing from the truth when Laney suggested my mother didn't care for her, but it's little things like this that only affirm her theory.

Meg leans in until our shoulders touch. "I've got my dancing shoes on. They're sure aching to get out there." She moves in another inch, hoping I'll put her feet out of their misery.

Meg. I shake my head. She's been my mother's shadow for the past few years while working as her personal assistant, but it's pretty clear I'm the one she's trying to assist, or, more to the point, my dick. Although she's already firmly stated she's waiting for her wedding night, and if she thinks I'm going to be the groom, she's got a whole lifetime of waiting to do because no matter what happens, no matter how desperately my balls plead for satisfaction, I'm not going there, ever.

Once Laney left, I quickly acclimated to the swollen hand blues, and, if need be, that's the way I'll continue to satisfy myself until I'm dead and buried. They'll find my skeletal hand right over my long-evaporated crotch.

I've only ever wanted Laney for as long as I can remember, and now that I have her for the night, I'm not sure what to do. Technically I'd be breaking my promise to "leave her the hell alone," but a cash transaction just took place for her time and attention, and I'm half-tempted to show her the receipt.

The cast moves through the crowd, mingling, laughing—breaking into spontaneous song as they grind past the patrons. Laney and Bing stick together as they circulate table-to-table, thanking everyone for coming out like they were guests at their wedding. My gut tightens just watching the way his hand touches her lower back like it belongs there.

Fucking Bing.

I pull my cheek back, pissed just witnessing the spectacle.

He twirls her to the table next to ours, and she manages to keep her back to me at all times. Laney has turned avoiding me into an art form. She could open up shop helping ex-girlfriends everywhere with effective techniques to steer clear of their ex's.

"You want to dance?" Meg strokes my hand and I rise out of my seat, half-afraid Laney will see her pawing at me. I'm equally afraid Laney and Bing will visit our table next, and she'll look through me like a ghost—hate me for sitting right next to the very girl she claims I destroyed our relationship over. It couldn't be further from the truth—ironic because I've always felt the truth would eventually come out and save the day, but I had no idea that it was capable of ebbing its way down the tree trunk of life slow as frozen tears.

Meg latches onto my elbow and tries pushing me toward the dance floor.

"No thanks," I bark, stern as shit. The last person on earth I'd dance with is Meg. It was the drama she caused that finally blew my relationship with Laney to bits. I untangle her limb from mine before she causes another unwarranted tragedy and head for the door.

Laney spins around just as I'm about to traverse an obstacle of seated gala patrons, and her chest lands soft against mine.

Holy shit.

Her beautiful face looks up at me, her breath blows over my skin as she pants. I'd like to think she was panting for me, from the excitement of being near me for the first time in months, but, in truth, she's been lit up like a pumpkin all night busy entertaining the masses, and that's always exhilarated her to the point of exhaustion.

Neither one of us moves, neither one of us says anything.

Her eyes key into mine, wide with anticipation, and I hold her gaze, daring her to move, to get the hell away from me like we both know she wants to.

Bing places his hand over her shoulder. "Cool. You got your date. Look, I've got a heated little slut waiting for me in the corner. She brought the big bucks, so I'd better head over and let her handle the merch." He socks me in the arm. "Don't do anything I wouldn't do." He glances down at Laney's chest. "If you're lucky, she'll let you sink your face in that hillside." He shoots me with his fingers before taking off.

Laney tries to take a step back, but I move right along with her and our bodies remain locked at the chest.

Truthfully I half-expected her to throw out some sarcastic comeback regarding her "hillside" like, *you won't be that lucky*, or *you'll never climb this terrain again,* and the fact she's chosen to remain silent only goes to show how virally pissed she still is.

I press my gaze into hers. "You want to dance?" There. Rules one and two have effectively been broken. Not only am I near her, but I'm speaking to her, touching her with my body in all the right places.

The music shifts to a Christmas carol with a rhythm far too quick to require our hips to bump and grind. Just my luck.

From the corner of my eye, I catch Roxy and Bryson's girlfriend, Baya, hedging their way over. If my sister knows what's good for her, she'll keep a safe distance. But as much as I'd like to believe I've got this handled, deep down I know Laney is about to flutter away, elusive as a butterfly, and I'll never have the chance to be near her again.

Laney's lids grow heavy as she skirts the table with a quick glance. You can feel the tension spewing from my mother, from Meg, and now all I want to do is get Laney the hell out of here, so I can protect her. In no way do I want anyone making her feel like crap, for sure I don't want to see anyone hurt her.

"You want to go to my place?" I can hardly believe I had the balls to make the offer. I moved just a week after Laney decided she wanted to break things off. It wasn't some reactionary situation, my lease was up and I had already secured the penthouse. Laney was going to see it as soon as I got the key, but she was long out of my life by then. And without her in it, the penthouse has been the loneliest place I've ever lived.

Her lips curl upwards, but she doesn't smile. Instead, she gives an exasperated sigh that cements the fact the only date I'm going to have this evening is the one with my hand later in the shower.

"How the hell did we end up here?" I whisper, mostly to myself because I half expect her to slap me and take off with Holt Edwards. I'd be lying if I didn't admit to envisioning the two of them lighting the sheets on fire, laughing their asses off at what a moron I've been.

Laney shakes her head ever so slightly.

"Laney Sawyer? Is that you?" Meg pipes up from behind, and the fact she's faking not knowing who this is, grates on me like a thousand fingernails clawing their way down a never-ending chalkboard. "Why don't you take a seat at the table with us?" She continues. "I'd love to catch up with you. I'm sure Mom would, too."

Laney twitches as if she were about to bolt—then she does the unimaginable.

Laney takes up my hand and whisks me right out the door.

My heart jumps into my throat. My dick ticks in my boxers because, holy hell, there's a tiny ray of hope that suggests he might get attention from the real deal tonight, but I think we both know that's a pipe dream.

The stars spray out over Hollow Brook like the breath of God—like magic—as Laney leads me into the parking lot.

It's a beautiful night, and I'm holding the hand of an even more beautiful girl. And, lucky for me, tonight might just hold enough magic for all of my pipe dreams to come true.

2

Love Shack

Laney

"Okay, I'll go to your place." I hear myself say.

"Okay?" Ryder looks slightly confused. His blue eyes expand the size of eggs, well, those expensive Russian Faberge eggs that sell for millions and have to be kept safe from the general population in heavy duty, guard-protected vaults.

Ryder Capwell is a rock star among men. I witnessed at least a half dozen girls readying to throw their panties in his direction before we chest bumped rather unceremoniously in front of Meg and his dear old mom. Really I couldn't think of a more thorough way to collectively piss them off, other than whisking him away to my sexual lair. I'm sure Mommy Dearest is gathering the wire hangers as we speak and fashioning them into my likeness.

"Yes," I breathe it out in a silver plume. The sky is crystalline, washed clean from last night's monsoon-like conditions. I've always been a sucker for a white Christmas, and seeing as how it's just days away, I'm sure we're going to get one. "I mean if the offer is still there." I'm still holding his hand, or at this point it's sort of vice versa because my fingers went limp the second we stepped outside, and his held on for dear life.

That bottle of whiskey I knocked back before hitting the stage has me feeling a little tipsy. I should seriously reconsider my antianxiety routine despite the fact it's given me the right amount of courage, or, more to the point, stupidity to engage in a conversation with someone who so horribly stomped on my heart.

"Hell, yes, the offer still stands." His chest pumps as if he just ran a marathon. He gives the impression of a smile, but his eyes remain fixed on mine—wide-eyed—as if he were lost in a dream.

"Hey!" Holt comes barreling out of the facility, and I take a quick breath because a part of me was expecting the Mommy and Meg breakup brigade to storm out after us. "What the hell?" Holt nods at our interlocked fingers. Holt is handsome, and sweet to boot, but he's not the one for me. I may have let him take me out a few times earlier this year when I specifically took to the task of bruising

Ryder's ego, but I felt bad for leading him on, so I broke things off before they could properly take off.

"I'm fine." I take a step back from Ryder, and our hands disconnect. "Would you mind telling my mom and sister I had to run?" I plead with Holt. "I think I'm going to turn in early."

He eyes Ryder like a snake in the grass, slithering its long phallic member ever so close to my forbidden forest.

"Yeah, sure," he says it stern with a threat embedded in the baritone of his voice. I've known Holt long enough to know he doesn't approve of me *turning in early* and with whom.

Ryder takes in a lungful of air as we watch Holt disappear back into the facility. "Laney," he whispers, touching his hand gently to my cheek. His eyes are narrowed in pain, his brows furrowed as if this were all too much for him. "Let's get out of here." A smile tugs on his lips as he takes up my hand again. He helps me into his sports car with its fresh from the factory scent, its dashboard lit up like the space station, and we don't say a word all the way over to Capwell Towers.

The ritzy high rise that bears the Capwell moniker is located in downtown Jepson which is about a half hour outside of Hollow Brook and a whole hell of a lot of walking miles from my dorm back at Whitney Briggs.

I'm such an idiot. Way to strand myself at my ex's place without my purse, which I stupidly left in a bag with all my street clothes. But, thankfully, I left both of those with Baya, so already I know I'll be seeing my wallet again, which is kind of a comforting thought.

"So, you ready to get your money's worth?" I sigh as we step into the glossy brass elevator and glide on up. His warm cologne washes over me, a heated spice with strong undertones of testosterone. I have the distinct feeling Ryder is about to put every dildo on the planet to shame with the things he's about to do to me, and I'm not too sure I'm going to protest the idea.

"You ready to give it?" He's teasing, mostly, but I can tell he's hopeful.

"Only in your dreams."

"Seeing that half my dreams have already come true tonight, I'm guessing the odds are in my favor."

Crap.

The elevator opens, and Ryder locks his aching navy eyes over mine. He's in physical pain, hurting so blatantly, and I don't know why I suddenly feel like everything that went wrong between the two of us was my fault. I'm not the one that left him naked in bed to help out a "friend."

Ryder steps into the hall, but I hesitate.

"I won't bite." His brows narrow like maybe he will.

My feet don't move.

"Maybe I want you to." What the hell am I saying? "Maybe I don't." Sadly, tucked somewhere in the middle lies the truth.

He holds the elevator open and dips his chin. "Come with me." It rumbles from him deep and sounds more like a sexual command than it ever does an invitation to see his apartment. "I promise, I'll only bite if you ask nicely."

"And if I don't ask nicely?"

A dark smile curls into his cheek. "That's when I ravage."

"Careful, cowboy. These heels are classified weapons in twelve different countries, banned in three, and I'm not afraid to use them." I take a breath and venture out onto the plush carpet that dampens the sound of my footsteps, making this feel even that much more of a bad dream.

"Duly noted." He strides alongside me. "By the way, have I mentioned that I have a strict no-shoes policy in the penthouse?"

"And how long has this been in effect?"

"Approximately twelve seconds."

"Lucky for me I have an affinity for breaking rules." I glance down at his crotch. "Put the boys on notice, the heels are coming in."

I revert my gaze to the ever-expanding walkway. The walls are covered with a creamy stone, while oversized wreaths decorate the long, narrow hall. The wreathes are white with bright red bows set in the center, and it looks festive in a sterile sort of way that only the filthy rich know how to pull off.

He holds out his hand, and I pause, eyeing it as if each finger were about to morph into a snake.

His dimples go off. "Again, I'll only bite if you ask."

"I'll take your hand, but only if you lower your oral expectations for the evening. I have a strict no biting policy I implemented about *fifteen* seconds ago, unless of course you've morphed into a vampire."

"Have I ever told you about that meaningful interview I had with Anne Rice several years back?"

"Very funny."

His fingers clasp onto mine and a sigh chokes from my throat.

How the hell did this happen? How did I travel miles across town only to end up alone with Ryder at his penthouse? Crap. The sudden urge to test out his mattress springs hovers over my head like the skanky ghost of

Christmas yet to come, and I think we both know the one really hoping to come is me. Why else would I have tagged along for the ride? To inspect his dinner dishes? God, I'm so stupid to have ever set foot in the car. This isn't going to end well.

"Everything okay?" He tightens his grip over my hand, and my face deepens a severe shade of crimson. I get lost in the bionic pull of his eyes, and, for a brief moment, everything actually does feel okay.

I'm quick to snap out of my Ryder inspired stupor. "Let's see, I was just auctioned off at a charity ball to my ex, I'm still bound and gagged in this seventeenth-century torture device once pawned off as fashion, and my phone, wallet, and dignity all went back to Whitney Briggs without me. My night, much like my life, just gave me the finger. But otherwise, yeah, everything's A okay."

Ryder pulls me in, raking his gaze over my features until my skin sizzles under his supervision.

"I'm not opposed to helping you out of that seventeenth-century torture device," he growls it out with the hint of a devious smile. "And if it makes you feel better, I'll leave my dignity at the door. We can indulge in hours' worth of undignified fun—comfortable, without our clothes on. If anything, I'm an accommodating host."

Holy holly-laden sleigh bells, this has quickly turned into the nightmare before Christmas. If I'm lucky this will pan out to be exactly that—one long nightmare—and the next thing you know, I'll be startled awake by my roommate gargling in the bathroom while I violently clutch at my choice weapon of mass destruction, my vibrator. Speaking of weapons, I probably should have one on me. Although, I think in this scenario, a revolver would be much more effective than packing a dildo. I don't think for a minute it's a coincidence that a penis is the shape of a .38 special—more like a Saturday night special. And considering this is Saturday night, I'd say his gun is about to be manhandled and fired and made to feel very, very special indeed because God only knows I've got a nice warm holster that I'd like to squeeze it into.

"I *bet* you're in an accommodating mood," it huffs from me incredulous. "I bet one very special part of you can't wait to accommodate yourself into a mind-numbing delirium."

His chest pumps once with a quiet laugh. "The only mind-numbing delirium I'd like to achieve is the one I hope to induce in *you*. Oh wait"—his dimples dig in and out—"we're back to oral fixations again, aren't we?"

Crap. It's like the walls are closing in on me with their spiny white wreathes, and I come to my senses. I pull free from his grasp, only Ryder doesn't seem to notice because he happens to dig into his pocket for the key at the exact same moment.

"Here we are." He swings open the door, and my eyes dart to the brass plated sign to his left that reads Penthouse 007.

"007?" I ask, disbelieving. Ryder is the only person I know that has the luck to have something as innocuous as his street address proclaim him as a badass. Well, would-be badass. I can't elevate him to that spectacular level after what he put me through.

He gives a cocky grin, and his dimples go off, rendering me and all of my hormonal girl parts defenseless.

"Capwell"—he gives the ghost of a smile—"Ryder, Capwell," he rumbles in his deepest octave, and my stomach pinches tight. "I've always wanted to say that." He smolders into me without even trying, and, good God almighty, I'm way past the point of being seduced. It's obvious this night is going to end with a bang, and now I feel like an idiot for putting myself within shooting, or rather bedding, range. Face it. Those cobalt eyes of his have cast a spell over me, and now, I'm voluntarily striding into his penthouse just hoping for some perversion.

He comes in close, and I'm terrified he's going to kiss me, and we'll be tearing off one another's clothes before I even get to berate myself properly for letting my vagina follow his happy trail right to his promiscuous penthouse.

"007!" I breeze past him before either of his heads can get within firing range. "That's quite impressive." I move into the living room at a lively pace as if I've got somewhere to go, as if I've been here before, then it hits me like a ton of cheating bricks—I bet *she's* been here before. "Do you lure all the women you purchase for the evening to your penthouse?"

God, could I get any closer to the point? Why not just shout out her name? I'm surprised I don't jump on his sofa and do a Tom Cruise in reverse, hopping up and down like a baboon shouting *I fucking hate Meg!* I do, though. I don't care how many charities she's commandeering. I couldn't care less if she's single handedly winning the war on poverty. I hate her yellow guts, her forked-tongue, and unspoiled liver because God knows that girl wouldn't have sucked down a fifth of whiskey before being auctioned off like a wench at some Disney theme-park attraction. But, then again, only in her wildest wet dreams would Ryder Capwell purchase her, let alone narrow his sexy gaze into her like he's doing to me now. I can practically feel him ravaging me with his eyes.

"Roxy is the only other girl that's been here." He presses out a dull smile at the mention of his sister's name. "She's visited twice. Not even my mother has set foot in these haunted halls." He brushes the hair from my face, and I can feel the flames fan from his fingertips. "Everything here, my *bed*, it's all been hoping you might show up," he whispers. "And here you are, Laney, just for me."

The sweet spot between my legs clenches when he says it, and I can feel the temperature rising around the two of us like an invisible inferno.

"It's nice to see you haven't changed—optimistic and egocentric as hell. Is that all you think it'll take to land me horizontal? A little purchasing power?"

"I don't think that's what brought you here. You're here because you want to be." He presses in an inch until his breath rakes over me. "And if I'm lucky, you'll be in my bed for the same reason."

I swallow hard and try to distract myself by taking in the place with its dark wood floors, the expensive Persian rugs in the dining and living room. The kitchen is a testament to stainless steel, and there's an art deco flair going on with clean lines, minimal furnishings. The Lshaped leather couch looks cold and uncomfortable. The television is the size of the wall and looks more like a black hole waiting to suck us in one-by-one, and right about now I wouldn't mind entering another dimension. Then the piece de resistance, a tall, blue Noble stands like a watchman in the corner.

"Ryder Capwell with a Christmas tree—fancy that." I step in further to inspect it with its plain red ornaments, dangling heavy as pomegranates, ready to plummet from the droopy branches. "I like it."

"Roxy's doing." He flips a switch, and the miniature lights go on in a rainbow seizure, blinking and winking, and, dear God, is that thing spinning? "She's got it rigged to sing and dance. It spins for hours, and somehow the wires never get tangled."

"That's the nice thing about electronics, you throw in a few batteries, they can satisfy you for hours—no wires, or feelings to get tangled up in."

A tangible silence crops up between us as Ryder gets that deer-in-the-headlights look knowing that I've replaced him with a sex toy.

"People are complicated, Laney." He steps in and sags, his face suddenly rife with grief. "And, I promise, there's not an electronic device in the world that can love you like I could if given a second chance."

"My broken heart would beg to differ. Besides, that's the nice thing about electronic devices, they don't need second chances—they get it right the first time."

"Maybe you should do a little juxtaposition?" His tongue glosses his bottom lip. "Conduct a side-by-side comparison by taking me for a test drive."

"Been there, done that."

"Maybe you need a refresher." He bears into me with an inescapable sorrow. I can feel his craving to have me, his carnal desperation—the eroticism pouring from his being as if he's unleashed the floodgates.

My chest heaves, my breathing grows erratic. Damn it all to hell because I'm right there with him.

I take a breath, turning back to the tree.

Somehow the holiday display endears me to him even if it was his sister's doing. And here I wanted to hate him. I wanted to relegate him to the cold, stainless, dark hardwood flooring, expensive Persian rug department where all the heartless bastards live and wipe the dust off my feet as I walked out the door. And now it's just so damn festive in here a part of me wants to curl up on the couch and stay the night.

"So what now?" I take a breath in anticipation. "You want to watch a movie—play a board game?" I meant to say that last part teasing, but it came out hostile, more like a threat. The truth is, I feel dizzy just considering the not-so-platonic options.

"No," he flat lines, somber. His eyes glaze over with his lust for me, and I can feel our bodies magnetizing toward one another like a coil that's been aching to retract for one long year.

Here I am, in Ryder Capwell's penthouse at the intersection of run-the-hell-away and lust-filled one-night stand.

"You want to give me the guided tour?" It's becoming painfully obvious to me what I'm doing here. And now I've no choice but to carry on with my subconscious desire to get him out of my system by way of inviting him into my body. It seems only logical. One good night in his arms—with his body buried deep inside me—and I might finally cull that incessant ache out of my heart—hell, out of my G-spot that's been weeping for him ever since he took his joystick and walked out of my dorm room all those lonely nights ago. This is my chance to have my way with him one last time. I can blame whiskey and every last dollar he donated to Whitney Briggs in my honor because God knows a whore like me wants to make sure he gets his money's worth.

Tears come unexpected, and I blink them away.

"Kitchen, dining room." He takes up my hand and speeds me down the hall. "Bathroom. Guest rooms." He picks up his pace and leads me through a set of double doors at the end of the hall to a luscious, horrifically oversized bedroom that could easily make the commons room at Prescott Hall feel inadequate. According to this cavernous space—the scope of his overgrown furniture—size very much matters to Ryder Capwell. "My bedroom." He locks his gaze over mine as the trace of a smile wafts on his lips. He's vexingly handsome in a dangerous way, still in his business suit. His silver tie gleams like a sword over his chest. "It's your move, Laney." He comes in close until his breath sears over my cheek. "It's a choose your own adventure kind of a night." He touches his finger to my chin and pulls my face up until I'm looking right into those ocean deep eyes. "What comes next?"

My heart rattles like a rabid beast trying to break free from its cage. My throat dries out, and my fingers shake because I've fallen past the point of no return and a one-night stand with my ex is clearly on the sexual horizon.

I reach up and loosen his tie. "You come next, Ryder." I pull him in like the tightening of a noose. "And if I'm lucky, I will, too."

Ryder

Laney Sawyer.

I stare at her in disbelief. A week ago, hell less than twenty-four hours ago, she wouldn't give me the time of day, and now, here she is, in a period piece costume from the drama department, looking every bit the nineteenth-century vixen.

"Are you propositioning me?" My body shakes, and yet somehow my voice manages to sail out smooth as velvet.

"Let's see." She cuts those denim eyes up at the ceiling, and I steal a glance at her perfect tits bulging from her corset. "I'm standing in your home—in *your* bedroom. You're the one with a hard-on pointed in my direction, so logic only insists that you, Ryder Capwell, are the one who is blatantly propositioning *me*."

A tiny laugh rumbles from my chest. I'd proposition Laney every day of the week if I knew she'd take me up on it.

She presses in closer as if she were making an offer.

Holy hell, the girl has a body that doesn't know it's defying both gravity and ten different laws of physics all at the same time. My fingers tremble for her, my hands shake like a crack addict who needs one more fucking hit, but I deny them the pleasure.

"You said my name." I let a lazy smile glide up my cheek. "You know it drives me insane when you say my name."

"That's because you have an insatiable ego."

I wait for her to follow it up with something far more reality-based like, *one that I plan on crushing soon*, but she doesn't.

"I'm going to be honest with you," I say as the smile slides right off my face. "I happen to think this is serious as shit." Her eyes widen. "I'm not sure how much more I can handle before I make a beeline for the bathroom to alleviate some of the pressure you've induced in me."

"My, my, you're quick to point the finger." She slips my tie off and runs it through her hand, nice and slow, as if she's about to teach both my dick and me a lesson.

"Just calling it like I see it." I wrap my hands around her waist, and she doesn't run screaming, so I take it as a green light and pull her in tight. My body molds over hers, and every cell in me sighs with relief. Laney is back, right here in my arms where she belongs. "You have two choices. Watch or help—and less than three seconds to decide."

"Only three?" Her neck arches back as she gurgles out a laugh.

"Two."

My hard-on knocks against her hip. I reach down to release my zipper, but she secures her hands over mine and shakes her head ever so slightly.

"Oh, believe me"—she whispers—"the pleasure is all mine."

"Be my guest."

Great. Her sarcastic piss and vinegar routine is pushing me over the edge whether I like it or not because I'm one hundred percent on board this crazy train. And to think, the last place I wanted to be tonight was at that auction. But here I am with Laney, running my fingers through her soft hair, and she's not pulling a weapon on me, so already I'm glad I showed.

"I think it's time for some altar worship." Laney drops to her knees, and that simple act has my boner trying to eject itself out of its casing. She works my zipper down, tugging at my clothes until both my boxers and pants are past my knees.

This is it. She's going to bite my dick off. I'd be a fool to think otherwise. I study her frame as she bows her head toward me. I'm pretty sure I could take her if I had to. But who the hell am I kidding? I'd let her bite my dick in half and offer up my balls for dessert. Just having her mouth around me one more time is enough to make me welcome a dickless death with open arms. Hell, I'd chop it off myself if I could get her to commit to sleeping with me just one more night.

Her lips brush over the tip, and I let out a guttural groan like a giant pussy because I still can't believe she's here. It's not some well-detailed hallucination, not some wet dream that I'm going to wake up from only to find that the bed is still empty.

Laney runs her tongue over the length of me, and I suck in a breath through my teeth. I push myself into her, just this side of begging her to put it in her mouth.

The logical part of me says pull away—stop before you both get into something you'll regret in the morning, or more to the point *she* will. She's drunk, or in revenge mode, and she'll Bobbitt me by sunrise if I'm not careful, but the primal part of me, the part that's having his balls molested by her cool fingers while her tongue strokes me back and forth like I was an erect piece of chocolate, just gave my logical half the finger.

"*Shit.*" I lean into her hard, hoping she'll take the hint and plunge me down her throat like a sword swallower.

Laney pulls back and looks up at me innocent and wide-eyed but in that bad acting kind of way that puts both me and my balls on notice. "Did you like that?"

"Yes," I choke out the word. "Laney"—I catch my breath—"why are you doing this?" And there it is. The pussy in me wins because we both damn well know she's up to something—that loving me tonight is simply a means to an end, most likely resulting in physical harm to her current point of interest.

"Because I miss you." Her expression dissolves to something just this side of tears as she glances back down at my dick still wagging in her face like the obscene tail of some happy-to-see-you canine. And, truthfully, that's about the long and short of it. I feel like an animal, like Laney's bitch in every single way, and, to be honest, I'd be whatever she wanted me to be if we could reenact this little scene night after night.

"I miss you, too." I run my fingers through her hair, like plunging through a silken waterfall. I used to spend hours doing just this while we watched TV, while we talked in bed, while I waited for her to fall asleep in my arms—and now here I am threading my fingers through her warm mane and yet nothing at all is how it used to be.

"I miss the way you taste in my mouth." Her lips glide over me, smooth and hot in one slick motion until she hits the base, and I let out a roar that's been bottled up in me for one year solid. Laney dives down over me again and again, and I writhe, grinding my shoes into the floor, twisting and turning, pulling her hair at the base of her neck and pushing her deeper into me. I'm spent. This is it. I've got another few good thrusts, and I'm going to explode, come for weeks, and there's nothing either one of us can do about it. But I stop short because I don't want this to be all about me.

"Come here." I hoist her up and hold my breath when I see her eyes swelling with tears. "Hey." I pull her in and my chest lurches because I'm this close to joining her in the tear-fest. "It's okay." I pepper her face with kisses, landing the sweetest one over her lips, and linger until her hot tears fall over my cheeks. I pull back and wipe them away. "You want me to take you home?" I touch my nose to hers a moment before bouncing back and taking in her beautiful features. Laney is as gorgeous as a runway model, and she doesn't even know it. That's part of her charm, she's humble and sweet and sarcastic as hell, but I wouldn't want her any other way.

She shakes her head and crashes her mouth over mine, violent and hungry. Laney very much wants this tonight, and as much as it breaks my heart, those tears reassure me that she still has feelings—that she's felt just as much sorrow and pain as I have, and it's all coming to a rolling boil tonight right here in my bedroom.

Something tells me, make-up sex at its finest is about to take place.

Laney rakes open my shirt and the buttons snap off as she rips it from my body. I pull off my clothes like stepping out of a fire. My fingers fumble with the back of her dress until I hit a zipper, and it snags about an inch of the way down.

I reach back and shut off the light, but she hits the switch and looks up at me with a renewed lust in her eyes.

"I want to watch." Her lips curl, and I think it's the first genuine smile I've seen all night—all year—and my heart sings at the sight of it.

"Then I'd better give you something to see." I lift her skirt, and my fingers find her bare waist. I groan into her as our lips make their way to one another again. Laney gently swipes her tongue over mine, and it feels like home. It feels as if my mouth, my teeth, my fucking tonsils have had every single one of their prayers answered because Laney Sawyer is right where she belongs—with me— falling into my mouth with her hotter-than-hell kisses. Gingerly, I back her toward the bed, only the room is so damn big it's turned into a moaning, loving, slow dance, and now, I'm about to write the builder a thank you letter for making the master bedroom so fantastically wide. My hands glide up her back, and I unhook her bra in some freshman maneuver I should be ashamed of, but this is Laney, and more than anything, I want her naked on my mattress so I can live out each and every fantasy I've had for the past three hundred and sixty-five days.

Laney reaches down and slowly unties her corset. Her eyes never leaving mine like a dare. She licks her lips before pulling her dress off in one Herculean move and leans against the bedpost, bearing herself to me in all her God-given glory. Her eyes widen as she licks the rim of her lips, flirting, tempting me to take a bite out of her in all the right places.

I cup her face and hold her like that while pouring my unspoken *I'm sorries* into her crystal cut eyes. I don't dare say the words. I don't dare bring up the past like the carcass it is. I don't want to clog up the room with the stench of all our sorrow. We're here now. I'm not so sure how we arrived, but there's not one part of me that wants to contest the logic.

I bow into her and press a searing kiss over her lips. I pull back and examine her like this in the light. Laney's dark hair falls across her shoulders, her perfect body expands and retracts in all the right places like an hourglass. I land a kiss in the hollow of her neck, lower still until I make my way to her nipple. My lips seal themselves over her, and I moan as her sweet, soft flesh conforms to my mouth. I roll my tongue over her nipple until she's hard, and my teeth graze her ever so gently until she gives a strangled cry.

I pull back and take her in. Laney looks up at me with her eyes slit to nothing, her neck arched back as she waits for more.

"Get in my bed," I whisper. "I'm going to love every last inch of you."

3

Let's Get it On

Laney

My legs clench as my body heaves with a little pre-orgasmic intent. Ryder has always held a cool command that drives women insane and makes them want to *get in his bed*—with me being the leader of the bed hopping bandwagon.

I glance down at his rock hard chest, then lower still and swallow hard. His erection is pointing at me as if picking me accusingly out of a line up as the perpetrator who tried to make off with his balls a moment ago. I'm sure his hard-on is screaming at the top of his testicles to get me to finish the job. I was more than ready and willing, but a very greedy part of me wants to extend the fun just a little bit longer.

My fingers fly up to his cut features, and I trace them out. I've known Ryder Capwell all my life, well, most of it.

Roxy attended my mother's dance school, and that's how we met. Ryder went to the expensive private school on the hill, so our meet and greets were far and few between in the beginning, but the older and wiser we grew, the more inseparable we became. A flashback of all those endless nights we spent wrapped in one another's arms gets caged in my mind, and I want to play them out on a loop more than I want to relive them. It was so much simpler back then, and now, there's a mile-wide heartache separating us emotionally. I'm not so sure falling into bed with him will ever fix that.

"Let's do this." He tightens his arms around my waist.

"Maybe I don't want to *get* in your *bed*," I say, and every last inch of me that he threatened to love into oblivion protests the idea of straying from his mattress. I hardly think my feet would listen if I willed them to carry me out of here. My primal instincts are in control of this party, and they scream *triple orgasms all around* as if they were buying. Clearly logic and reason aren't invited tonight.

Ryder lowers his lids, rendering me defenseless to his bedroom eye superpowers. His features harden as if I've blatantly pissed him off and he was about to teach me a lesson. He dips his thumbs into my panties and hitches them below my hips until they voluntarily fall to the ground.

"Would you look at that?" he whispers over my lips without taking his eyes off mine. "Here we are, naked in my bedroom."

"Hard to believe." I run my finger over the length of him when I say it.

"I want you back, Laney." His jaw redefines itself as his hand finds that tender part of me that's been screaming out for him ever since that last night we were together. I let out a heated breath because I'm finding it impossible to focus on the finer details of our breakup while he rubs me into a sexual nirvana. Maybe a little revenge sex is what I really need. One wild night to work him out of my system—maybe then I'll finally be free.

I wrap my arms around his neck and touch my forehead to his chest. My body writhes to the rhythm of his magical fingers. It's obvious now that an entire suitcase full of vibrators could never replace the real deal.

I arch my neck back and let out a groan. "The thing I mourned most was the fact our bodies never had the chance to say a proper goodbye." It sails from my lips in a hoarse whisper. "Maybe that's what this is, one long, drawn out, carnal goodbye." I look up at him because a small part of me wants him to refute the theory.

"Goodbye?" He presses out a dull smile while studying me with those dark unknowable eyes. "This isn't goodbye." He gravels it out with demonic intent. "What you're about to experience is wild, savage make-up sex."

"You're forever the optimist." My heart thumps because I sort of like the idea of make-up sex a whole hell of a lot better. For a moment I envision us snuggled up by the fire as we throw fistfuls of dildos into the flames because with Ryder around there's no need to keep spare man parts hidden in my underwear drawer.

"Let me love you." He strokes the hair from my face. There's a tenderness in his voice, in his eyes, that I haven't seen in so long. I want to believe it's real, but a part of me can't be sure. This is just the homerun at the end of some bizarre night at a charity ball. A cash exchange took place, and he was simply accepting my services. This means as much to him as the tax donation that landed me here in the first place.

"I don't think you know how to love me, Ryder," I give it in less than a whisper. Sometimes it's hard to hear someone tell you the truth, but it's also hard to be the one to say it.

"I do. Let me into your heart, Laney," he pleads with those deep navy eyes as we stand just shy of his bed. "Let me crush every memory you have of the two of us and make something new, something better, something that never disappoints because it doesn't know how." He dots a series of hot kisses slowly up my neck, and a shiver runs through me.

My skin touches his, and then it's over. I'm all in. Every last inch of me has been so thirsty for Ryder, and now, here I am, ready to drown in the cool spring of his affection while my entire body reanimates under his willful supervision. A part of me died last winter in a very real way, and, here he is, reawakening me, breathing life back into my soul by way of his mouth, his fingers—his bare flesh.

He pulls back and rakes over me with his slow gaze.

"Get in my bed," he growls it out, sharp like an order.

"If you want me in your bed, you'll have to damn well put me there yourself."

Ryder gives the ghost of a smile.

And he does.

Ryder scoops me into his arms and lands me on the cool comforter. He glides over me, and my skin ignites like a field fire. Our fingers interlace as he pushes my hands high above my head. Ryder parts my legs with his and settles his body in the gap while his tongue takes free roam of my mouth.

I give an involuntary moan as my hips rise into him as if my vagina had just delivered a formal invite to the general and two colonels to invade my fort any time they damn well pleased—right fucking now would be nice. I claw at his back, raking my way down his granite-like ass and digging in, hoping to hurt him the way he hurt me. Of course, my injuries were emotional—a battered heart, a tattered ego. I could never hurt Ryder where it really counted—not sure I would want to.

His kisses grow erratic and sloppy as he traces his hot tongue all the way over to my ear.

"You want me to fuck you, don't you?"

Ryder always did like to get to the point.

"Yes," I choke it out because as much as my dignity wishes it could strangle me, my body would much rather have one last night of rough sex with an ex than sit alone and wallow in my righteousness.

"Too bad." He breathes it hard in my ear as he settles his weight over me. Ryder presses in a slow, circular kiss over my lips until my insides buzz with delirium. "I'm not fucking you ever again, Laney. I'm going to make love to you, forever if you'll let me." He continues his kissing assault down my neck, and my heart melts at his sweet sentiment.

Tears spring to my eyes, and I'm quick to blink them away. This is nothing more than a one-night stand. I can't buy into the lies Ryder is feeding me. I wasn't enough for him or his family just a few short months ago—I don't see why I would be now.

Ryder dips his kisses into my cleavage. He pushes my breasts together and buries himself in the mass of flesh. His groans are far more viral than I remember. I try to memorize each tug and pull, the way his teeth graze over my nipples, the hot of his mouth as it works me into a heated daze. He grazes lower still, raking a line down my torso with his molten hot mouth. His tongue unleashes on my belly, and my toes curl from the quivering sensation.

Holy hell.

There should be a one-night stand emergency response necklace they force girls to wear in college. Only instead of having some medical staff on standby it would be an entire legion of girlfriends who were more than capable of handling a sexual distress call. I can envision it now—me hitting the magic button until Roxy and Baya pop up on the other line. *Help, I've fallen in bed with my ex, and he's gotten* it *up. He's hedging his way to the runway with his motherfucking tongue, and I am completely immobilized. Send help by way of*

distractingly cute Whitney Briggs football players, hell—
send the entire team!

Who the heck am I kidding? It's more like send provisions. I plan on keeping Ryder's tongue busy for quite some time, until morning to be exact.

I had a shift tonight at the Black Bear, but Baya will have to hold down the fort for me. I'm too busy doing what I swore I would never do again—letting Ryder sink his wickedly sexy mouth in places no mouth has ever traveled. Well, except his. He's no stranger to the hills and valleys, the canyons and mountains of this girl's terrain. He knows my every nuance, what the pattern of my breathing means, he knows how to distinguish each and every kiss I give him, and he knows how to pleasure me in ways that I never knew were possible.

Ryder gently lifts my legs until they're sitting over his shoulders and parts my thighs just enough to enjoy the view.

He melts his lips over the most intimate part of me, and I let out a cry, knocking my head back into the pillow. There he is. Taking up residency in the holy of holies. I swore I'd never let him near me again, but tonight is proof positive that I'm weak, that whiskey makes me more than a little fucking frisky and auctioning myself off like some turn-of-the-century wench is always, *always* a piss poor idea.

He moans before pulling away and moving his sleepy eyes back up to mine. I hike up on my elbows, out of breath, and pant into him for an unreasonable amount of time.

Stupid, stupid me for insisting the lights stay on.

I want to *watch*? Watch what? The unflattering way my boobs roll to my armpits when I lie back instead of perking to the ceiling? It's like my nipples turn into a couple of lazy eyes that drift to the mattress, making me look unnecessarily flat chested. I'm half tempted to hold them into position all night, but I'd much rather dig my fingers through his hair.

His lips curve just enough to give him that dangerous appeal that made me gravitate to him to begin with.

"What the hell are you smiling at?" I thump my knee over his bottom. "Get back to work."

His brows peak in that dark, seductive way that makes my toes curl all on their own.

"Was I smiling?" His eyes continue their viral assault on my hormones, and I'm about to have a double orgasm without the satisfaction of having it derived from his lips.

"Damn straight you're smiling because you and I both know it's your lucky day." Did that just fly out of my mouth? God, I love it when the whiskey talks, and takes off my clothes, and lands me in bed with the exact person I swore to never speak to again. Note to self, make shrine to whiskey before setting the whole damn bar on fire for housing the promiscuous poison.

He huffs a dull laugh. "Oh, sweetie, this isn't work. This is a pleasure cruise." His hand travels down past my hips as his fingers trace out my wet folds. He plunges a finger into my body and works his thumb over me in a circle.

A swell of anger fills me from out of nowhere, and I'm beginning to think whiskey is code for mild psychosis. "*First*, I'm nobody's 'sweetie,'" I correct him a little more throaty than intended. Although, I'm not so sure how one goes about critiquing the distribution of an orgasm, but seeing that I'm in bed with my ex, no level of evil is off the table tonight. "And *second*—there are a lot of things your hands are good for, trust me, this isn't one of them. If it's one thing that makes me testy it's being made to endure waning fireworks only to be denied the grand finale."

"Waning fireworks?" he mouths.

That vexingly hot grin crops up on his face, his chin dips with wicked intent.

"Listen, *honey,*" he growls it out alarming sexy, and my sweet spot starts in on a series of spasms. Crap. I knew the big O was knocking at the door. "The only thing waning is my dick, and I'm about to find it a nice, wet home." He extracts his finger from deep inside me, and my insides wail to have him back. His features soften as he holds my gaze. "I love you, Laney." His perfect lips twist, the muscles in his jaw pop. He's waiting for me to say it back. His eyes latch onto mine and make sweet love to me all on their own. He rides his wet hand up my belly and strums over my flesh just begging to hear those words, but I won't give them. That's not what tonight is about.

And, perhaps, that's not what we've ever been about.

"To work," I say.

He growls before dipping down between my legs and burying a kiss over me. His tongue lashes out, loving yet violent.

"Oh God." I grip the bedding and clutch at it as if I were in pain. A cry rips from my throat, and I lurch forward with my fingers knotted in his hair. My body responds without hesitation, and I spasm right into him.

I do love Ryder.

But I'll be damned if those words ever leave these lips   again.

Ryder

I close my eyes and lounge over the sweetest part of Laney's body, loving her, molding my mouth over her while soaking in all the heated moans, the nail-digging groans. I'm savoring the taste, the way her legs cascade up and down my back, the way she's pulling out my hair, hard, just this side of violent, but I don't really give a shit if I walk away battered, bruised, and bald. It's as if all of time had shrunk down to this tiny microcosm, and here we were again, a place I never thought we'd get to. I sink down lower and penetrate her with my tongue, spinning spirals through her again and again, half-afraid to stop because I don't know if I'll ever get the chance to visit here again.

"*Ryder.*" She grinds into me, and I bury a kiss over her. "Ryder, *please.*" Laney coils her fingers around my hair and pulls me up a few inches. She's panting and writhing, and I can't help but dig a smile in my cheek. For so long this is what I've wanted, and now that I have it, I don't plan on denying either one of us a moment of pleasure. I lunge over her, lashing her with my tongue, harder, faster than she needs it until her breathing sounds erratic and her knees lock over my skull like a vice. "Ryder!" She bucks forward and holds me captive right where I want to be. I'd volunteer to be Laney Sawyer's sex slave if she'd have me. This headlock right here is the reward I'd live for each and every day. I'd rearrange my world to have Laney back in my life. And, if she gives me the chance, I'll do just that.

"Come here, you." She pulls me up, and I fall over her in a heated slick. I hike up on my elbows and take in the rosy glow of her cheeks. It's satisfying to know I put that beautiful pink color in her face—that I still have the capability to light her up from the inside—that she'd let me.

"Damn you're beautiful, you know that?" I stroke the hair from her forehead. "You're drenched from head to toe, and we're just kicking off the party."

"Says who?"

"My hard-on." I take her hand and guide it over me until her fingers clasp on, and I flinch as if she kicked me in the gut.

"Maybe that was my wicked plan all along." She rolls back, and her body glistens in the light. "Get what I can then get the hell out."

I groan into her. "I can live with that."

"You can?" She readjusts her head on the pillow as her paper-white teeth graze her cherry-stained lip.

"Why don't you come by night after night and test me?" I swallow hard. "I'd die happy knowing I'd get to end each day with you raining down your perfect pleasure right into my mouth."

She gives an impish grin. "You're a dirty boy, Ryder." Her lips quiver. Laney's expression takes a turn for the serious. Her eyes round out, vulnerable and sweet like a little girl. "I've missed you." She gives a hard sniff into my neck and lets loose with the tears.

"Laney." I swallow hard while pressing a kiss just above her ear. I reach over to the nightstand and switch off the lamp. The lights from the Christmas tree pour into the room and cover us in a kaleidoscope of color. "I missed you, too." I sink down next to her and wrap my arms around her. "I'm never letting you go." My voice cracks, and I don't really care if I sound like a pussy. "We're going to make this work. My world doesn't function the way it's supposed to without you. I can't take the fucking pain one more minute." I press my lips hard over hers and she reciprocates with an explosive kiss that threatens to combust the entire damn room.

Laney runs her hands down my back and rounds out to the front. She strokes my dick, guiding it. Her other hand gently grazes my balls until the need to have her takes over.

I reach back onto the dresser in what's proving to be more of a ceremonious maneuver since I know for a fact I don't have any protection lying around—there hasn't been a reason, and, now, I feel like an idiot for having the girl of my dreams ready and willing, and here I am, unable to dive in like I want.

"Crap." I lie back on the bed, disbelieving that my wildest dreams are about to come crashing to an end because I can't for the life of me remember where the hell I have a missile shield stored.

"What's the matter?" She props up on her elbow and traces my body out with her eyes.

"I'm sort of out of raincoats."

"Is that all?"

"That's a pretty big deal." I give a bleak smile. A part of me is hoping she'll surprise me with the fact she's on the pill, and I can dive in anyway. I'm starting to get the shakes, like a starving man who's crawled on his belly through the long, hot desert only to find a glass divide between him and the gourmet meal he's been salivating after.

"It's not a big deal." She lands her finger over my chest and creates a giant letter S as she sizzles her way down to my weeping dick. "I'll take care of you."

I pull her onto me and feel the weight of her sweet tits over my chest.

She lowers her head until our lips collide. Laney chases me with her tongue as I pour all of my affection straight into her mouth.

I pull back and steady my gaze over hers.

"I'm insanely, deliriously, outright fucking crazy in love with you. Laney"—I swallow hard because I'm going there—"take me back."

If she did—if we could work things out—it would make what she's about to do that much sweeter. Just knowing she loves me, that she's willing to open her world to me once again would bring Christmas a little early, not that she hasn't already done that. I guess it would be the star on the tree.

A lone tear falls from her cheek to mine.

"I..." She takes a breath as if I caught her off guard. "I need some time to think." She presses her lips together hard. "You know what happened, Ryder. You were there. This is complicated and..." She buries a kiss over my neck, and now I want nothing more than to end this conversation. Laney's chest bucks with silent tears. She gives a hard sniff as if she were checking her emotions.

"It's all right." I run my hand over her smooth hair and take in her vanilla scent. There's no way it's all right, but the last thing I want is to upset her any more than I already have. I should have known she wasn't going to fall over me with an enthusiastic yes. This was far too twisted, too many people have trampled between us, and as much as I hate to admit it, she's right. This is complicated.

Laney trails slow, blistering kisses straight down my body. She runs her fingers across my chest as if she were mapping out the landscape. I want to tell her she doesn't have to do this—that given five minutes in the shower I should have things under control, but I don't. The truth is, I want this from her, from her hands, her mouth. Nothing compares to the way she loves me, and for damn sure not one part of my body can substitute what Laney can give me.

Her mouth lands over the tip, and I let out a heated breath.

"Right there." I hike up on my elbows and bend my head back just taking in the sweet feel of her lips. Laney opens up and devours me, carefully raking her fiery tongue over my body as she slips me back out of her mouth. She dives down and wraps her lips tight around me, sucking as if she were about to inhale me, dick first, into her body. "*Shit*," I belt it out, and the room vibrates.

Laney drops down, running her tongue over my balls, and my stomach clenches.

"Yeah that." My chest pumps with a dry laugh.

I don't ever remember her employing these moves. She brings her hand to the party and works her fingers over me in a place where fingers or any other body parts are never allowed. I try to deflect her, and she catches me by the wrist. Her mouth melts back over me, riding me in a wave of insanity, and I'm about to lose it.

Laney works her magic while doing her best to suck me down to nothing. She takes me in all the way to the base, and I fucking lose it. Laney doesn't move, she just drinks me down like some tropical cocktail, and I lurch forward with a roar ripping from my lungs until the shakes subside.

Laney climbs up and falls back next to me on the mattress. We just stare up at the ceiling for moment, wondering what the hell just happened.

"Come here." I pull her in, and she collapses her heated chest to mine. "You okay?" I know for fact she's never swallowed before. At least not me, and I hope to God she hasn't been practicing while we've been apart. God knows a year of celibacy nearly killed me, but just the thought of Laney loving anyone else with that body would test my mortality and the mortality of the one she slept with.

"Why wouldn't I be okay?" She rakes her fingers through my hair with a renewed tenderness. All of the primal tendencies she held just a few minutes ago have been quenched at least that's what I'm hoping. "I'm fine."

"Thank you." I touch my finger to her cheek and trace out her immaculate bone structure, her pillow-soft lips.

"For what?" She buries a kiss in my palm.

"For loving me."

"Who said I loved you?" She dips her chin, never taking her gaze off mine.

"You didn't have to tell me." I pull her in, and she twists until we're spooning. "You showed me."

Laney sighs into me, pulling my arm tight across her waist.

Here we were after thoroughly loving each other—mostly—after tears and every emotion known under the sun, and we were pushing through. Riding the edge of the night with our bodies tangled as one.

Nothing could be better.

Nothing could ever come close.

4

The Way We Were

Laney

The sun filters in through a crack in the curtains, and I startle because I can't make out the layout of my bedroom. I give a series of rapid blinks, dizzy and bleary-eyed at my foreign surroundings. The dresser is bigger...and why is the door on the other side of the room? I lean up on my elbow and squeeze my eyes shut tight once again until the room warbles in and out of existence. The door, the dresser, the man breathing heavily next to me—

I seize the sheet over my naked body and slide in the opposite direction a good two feet.

Crap! I let out a little squeal as I give a one-eyed stare over at the penis slinger snoring next to me. Last night comes crashing back like an avalanche of spinning Christmas trees and blowjobs, and I groan as I dread to face my new reality. I glance at him with his dark rumpled hair, his strong wide back turned toward me.

Dear God let that be Ryder.

I hope to God I didn't hallucinate last night with some not-so-close second and pretended to be having sex with my ex while sucking down the man juice of some drunk fifty year old I picked up at the Black Bear.

I kick him in the thigh, and he obediently rolls over exposing the fact that the penis slinger snoring next to me is very much sexier-than-hell Ryder Capwell, and thankfully so, or I'd have to tiptoe the hell out of here while clutching my costume like a toddler.

It all comes back to me with perfect clarity. Whiskey—that stupid, *stupid* auction.

I glance over at him once again. There he is, in his immaculate state of early morning duress. I'm guessing that tent peg lifting the sheets at his crotch is exactly how he plans on saying good morning.

My fingers glide to my throbbing forehead and I sigh because, for one, I'm not safely tucked in Prescott Hall—hell, I'm nowhere near Whitney Briggs, and a wild fear grips me. I could call a cab but I don't have my wallet. I could call Baya or Roxy, but I don't have my phone, and God knows I don't have anybody's number memorized.

Ryder turns into me, and his hands swipe for my waist. Something in the motion—in that subconscious act brings back all those old feelings, and I break. I scoot in and let his arm find me, scooping me next to him like I belong there. His snoring ceases as he latches on and the touch of a smile glides over his lips. I want to say something, kiss him, or wrap my hand around that early morning greeting of his that's scraping against my thigh. But if I remember correctly, we're down one protective hedge and about a fifth of whiskey.

Then on cue, my head begins to throb as if the sun itself had detonated in my skull. I rub my temples for a moment.

"No, no, *no*," I moan.

"Yes, yes, *yes*." He pulls me in by the small of the back until my chest crushes against his and lands a hot morning kiss over my lips. I don't hesitate to take more than he's giving and plunge my tongue into his searing mouth. What the hell, I've already crossed every imaginary line in the sand, and, somehow, over the course of the night my heart thawed out, and all of those wonderful feelings I once had filled in the reserve like a bright spring morning.

Ryder tastes sweet, juicy, and something about the way he's manhandling my boobs has me panting for a reprisal of just about every activity we shared last night.

I pull back, my lids heavy with a renewed lust for him.

"I don't think I ever want to leave." I bite down over my lip to stave away the tears because in reality very few things have changed, and yet we've unwittingly opened another door.

"Lucky for you because I wasn't planning on letting you go." He warms my arms with his hands. "Stay." He pleads with those midnight blue eyes. "Let me cook you breakfast. I make a mean omelet, and I have every intention on making those Mickey Mouse pancakes you love so damn much."

I give a little laugh as I tighten my grip around his waist. "I can't stay. I have rehearsal at noon."

"Tell them you're sick."

"That's bad luck."

"Tell them you're too busy getting your insides licked, and they can all go to hell—starting with Guy Richards."

"Ryder!" I slap him across the chest as a laugh gets buried in my throat. "That's crude."

"Yeah, but you loved it." He lays his head over mine and snuggles into me.

"I did." I sigh into him. "I loved a lot of things you did—that you said last night."

I run my fingers through his dark hair, and our eyes lock. Ryder Capwell has an entire ocean hostage in those deep navy eyes.

"Let me love you, Laney. Don't walk out of my life again." His Adam's apple rises and falls. "I can't handle it. I need you here just to breathe."

Crap.

I swallow hard. I'd like to think it were as simple as me saying yes—that suddenly things would change for the better, but the reality is, all those old issues would be right there waiting for us again. They're haunting us even now, waiting for us to just try and make things right so they can hack us to pieces all over again.

"Tell me what to do, Laney." He lets out an exasperated breath. "Tell me who to cut out of my life, and I'll do it."

I dart my gaze into him as his words settle in my stomach like battery acid.

"I never asked you to cut anybody out of your life." I hack the words through the air, jagged and careless. They slice right through any magic last night might have carried and expose this morning for what it is, the day after something that we'll soon regret.

Ryder spikes up on his elbows, his features soften.

"That's not what I meant." His dimples dig in and out as he runs his tired gaze over me. "I'm serious, Laney. I'm in this for the long haul. There is nobody else that I care to keep in my life if it means I can't have you. Don't push me away." He wraps his arm around me and lands a kiss over my shoulder. "Just let me love you."

It's tempting. I'm caving I can feel it, but that residual anger surges like a tidal wave.

"If you want this so bad, why make me choose who you're going to spend your time with?" I shake my head while doing a quick scan of the floor for my dress. At this point I couldn't care less about my underwear. Hell, I might even call the shoes a loss.

He secures his arm around my waist before I can even think of rolling out of bed. I glance back at him. Ryder is so damn handsome in this early morning light with his rumpled hair, his laser blue eyes pressing into me with something just this side of an intrusion. His cheeks are peppered with stubble, and it gives him that undeniably gorgeous look. Ryder Capwell is sex on a stick. Any woman on the face of the earth would give her right boob to be in my position.

"I've already chosen who I want to spend my life with." A tiny dimple appears on his left cheek. "It's you, Laney, it's always been you. I'm sorry for every stupid thing I've said and done. From the bottom of my heart I beg your forgiveness." His features harden as if he's holding back tears.

A moment of silence stops up the air. Here it is, the fork in the relationship road. Go with Ryder or go home and hope you have enough AA batteries to reenact those wild stunts his tongue pulled off last night. Our eyes latch, and he winces as if pleading. My heart melts at the sight of him, at the thought of him wanting me just as bad as I want him.

"Okay," I whisper, taking back my wrist.

"Okay?"

"I won't cut you out of my life, Ryder." I cup the side of his face, and he turns into me with a kiss. "I want this with you."

"Laney." His brows pitch, giving him that demonically sexy look I've missed so much. "Thank you." He touches his forehead to mine, exhaling his relief over my chest. His breathing picks up pace. His eyes glisten with tears. Ryder melts his mouth over mine and pulls me over his body. We fall into a world of deep, soulful kisses—long, primal, animalistic, I'm-so-hungry-for-you tongue lashings, and, best of all, kisses that brand the words I love you over one another's hearts better than words could ever do.

Sometimes you need to say things with actions, you need to show one another that the inherent promises a relationship entails are going to be kept. That when you give your heart away, the person you give it to will protect it at all costs. Every girl dreams of being loved with an unquenchable fire—and the only person who I'd want that combustible affection from is right here next to me, lighting up the sheets.

I want my forever with Ryder Capwell and hope this time we can find a way to make it happen.

Something tells me it won't be as easy as we would like it to be.

⊰⊱

The long drive back to Whitney Briggs isn't nearly as awkward as I imagined. Before we left, I showered alone despite a rather lengthy plea on his part. But I figured with all that slipping and sliding going on, I might be tempted to impale myself on his eminence and what with no protection around, things were bound to get procreative on us. Not that I'd mind having Ryder's dark-haired, drop dead gorgeous children with their dimpled smiles, their midnight eyes. He's one stud I'd gladly sacrifice the size of my uterus for. But I think we should take it one life event at a time, starting with the renewal of our relationship.

"So what's the game plan for today?" I ask as the road stretches out in front of us like a long asphalt tongue. Everything in me cries out to have Ryder again. It's all I can do to keep from taking the wheel and landing us in a ditch. I can't help but notice that the world outside our windshield is giving off its own sexual projection. The evergreens spear the sky with their phallic protrusions. The rolling hills round out like a series of melon-like breasts that ache for a kiss from the horizon. The steel grey clouds look down over creation, heavy with anticipation, ready to release all of their frustration in one trembling thrust.

"No game plan. I'm with you." Ryder picks up my hand and lands a simple kiss over the back. "That's all I need to know. You sure you need to get to rehearsal? I've got a pretty good idea of where I can pick up those raincoats." He nods to a gas station on our right.

I give a little laugh. *Raincoat* used to be our code word for condoms. Of course, I went on the pill to surprise him last Christmas, but we never got to the surprise. His mother and Meg made sure of that. But I've been on it ever since. I don't know why I didn't tell him last night. I guess, deep down, I wanted to make sure we were solid again, but, then, we were never solid to begin with. I suppose if I'm going to let a man rain down on my insides, I'd better be sure he's the one. I glance over at Ryder in his dress shirt and jeans, his heavy wool coat on over that. He's so gorgeous that a part of me demands we pull over so I can crawl onto his lap and let him take me right here in the field like a rabbit.

I press out a dull smile. Maybe I will tell him. Maybe that will be my gift to him on Christmas Eve. God knows I don't have the funds for something far more tangible like a sweater or a tie. But I'm guessing he'd surrender ever wearing a sweater or tie again for the intimacy I'm about to gift him with.

We pull into the student parking lot, and he finds a spot closest to the entry near Prescott.

"I'll take that as a no as far as the raincoats go." He reaches over and tweaks my knee.

"More like a rain *check*."

"Come home with me tonight." His eyes hold mine with the slight patina of desperation. Ryder is still afraid I might scatter like a timid bird, and a part of me wonders the same thing.

"I have a show tomorrow night." I interlace our fingers and rub my thumb over his palm. I'm ready to cave—so close.

"I promise I'll get you back on time."

"I have no doubt." I reach up and touch my hand to his stubble. "What I'm afraid of is the fact I won't get any sleep."

"You got me there." He plants a kiss over the back of my hand. "Sleep is nowhere on the agenda, but if you insist, I swear I'll be content just holding you." His dark brows swoop in as if to confirm his quasi-vow of celibacy. The truth is, I miss sleeping in Ryder's arms. I haven't had a decent night's sleep in a year, and that's because he wasn't there to hold me.

"You may be content with simply catching some shut eye, but I won't." I bite down over a naughty smile. We get out, and he comes around to my side. His arms find themselves a home around my waist as if it were the most natural thing in the world. "I want all of you, Ryder." The crisp air cuts through my dress like knives as I shiver into him. "I want you in every possible way, all night long. I want to feel you deep inside me. I never want to be apart from you again."

His stomach flinches beneath me. Ryder cradles my face in his hands and presses out a sad smile.

"Laney. We're back." He sweeps his gaze over each of my features as if memorizing the moment. "And I promise you, we're never going to be apart again."

He brings his lips to mine, and we share a kiss right here at Whitney Briggs in front of the roaming eyes of the student population. It's freeing, blissfully familiar—desperately hungry—it's as if Ryder had been off at war, and now I have him back again. But the war was of our own making. The battle lines were drawn by his mother, and I wonder how long we can stand again before she topples us over for good. I know for a fact I'm the last person she wants to see her son with, and that alone makes me wonder if this is all a big mistake. Can our love really survive anything?

Good God, I hope so.

ଧ୍ୟଓଷ

Ryder takes off to look for Bryson. He asked if he could share our big news, so, of course, I said yes. I spin in a quiet circle as I head over to Prescott in my oversized, ratty Madame Thenardier ball gown. I still have an hour before I need to be at dress rehearsal. I'd like to hit my dorm room and process everything that's happened. A part of me still can't believe I spent the night with Ryder just like that, out of the blue.

"Laney!" A girl's voice shrills from my right, and I spot Baya and Roxy huddled under a space heater outside the café.

I give a little squeal and head on over.

"Look who decided to roll out of bed?" Baya pulls up a seat for me as I join them. It's freezing out, after all it is December and the threat of a serious storm is hovering above us.

Baya slides over my bag. I pluck my phone out and clutch it like a missing child. There's a text from Mom.

Christmas Eve, my house. Don't bring the twerp.

I slip the phone back into my purse, lest Roxy see that my mother has resumed the name-calling.

My mother never was one to mince words. I have a feeling even if Ryder and I never split, she still wouldn't approve of him. She's made a hobby of nitpicking at my life decisions ever since I quit working for her dance studio years ago. Izzy is still there. But, then, if she praised me like she does Izzy, I'd probably still be there too.

"So?" Roxy stirs her coffee before plucking out the svelte red straw. "Did you roll out of bed *alone*?"

"Of course, she didn't." Baya plucks at my pillowy sleeve. "It's obvious we're witness to the walk of shame."

"Is this true?" Roxy wants to hear it straight from my lips.

Of course, Baya is much quicker to believe me. She doesn't know all the gory details of what happened last year, and Roxy, unfortunately, does.

"It's true. But we didn't quite go all the way." I throw in that last part in a weak attempt to save face. After all, I did threaten to slit my own throat should I ever find myself horizontal with Roxy's brother again.

I shoot a quick glance out at campus as a heat wave from last night's lovemaking rolls through me. I can still feel his tongue lashing me in places I've only dreamed of for the entire solid year.

"Told you." Roxy jabs her straw at Baya. "They're not like the rest of us. They've got some serious underlying issues they can't get past." She shakes her head as if she's glad she's not me, and she should be.

"We tried to go all the way, but we were lacking in the protection arena. You know what they say, *especially in December, wrap your member*. We'd like to hold off on the breeding until sometime after graduation."

"You're back together?" Roxy's mouth falls open, and she's quick to slap her hand over it.

"No." I squeeze my eyes shut. "I mean, yes. We still have some kinks to work out, but I think maybe this time we can get there."

"That's great!" Baya pulls me into a spontaneous hug. "I'm so happy for you. I can't wait to meet him. He seems like a really nice guy from what I can tell."

"Ryder is the best." Roxy presses her lips together like she might cry. "So, these kinks...do they involve my mother?" Roxy knows full well they do.

"I'm sorry." I glide my hand over her arm. "But things have to change, or I just can't be a part of Ryder's life."

She glances down at the table, mournful as to what it might mean.

"Look"—my heart starts racing, and it feels like I'm right back at that party last Christmas Eve—"she doesn't have to like me. She doesn't even have to acknowledge my presence when we're in the same room. But if I'm going to be with your brother, I need her to respect that and not throw other girls at him. And, if I had my way, she wouldn't badmouth me either."

"I guess that won't be a problem now." Roxy pulls her sweater over her fingers and shudders at the idea.

Roxy and I let the silence bleed in and as we gaze morbidly at one another. We both know Ryder made some veiled threats about cutting his family out of his life if we ever got back together. He made them last year and hinted at it again this morning.

"What's going on?" Baya waves her hand over our faces like she's trying to pull us out of a trance.

"Nothing's going on." I let out a sigh, and a plume of fog expires from me. "I'm not trying to destroy your family, Roxy. I promise you. That's exactly why I stepped out of the picture last year. Anyway"—I shrug into Baya—"it's really complicated."

"I don't get it." Baya darts her lime green eyes from me to Roxy. "How's it going to destroy your family if your mother is the one who keeps saying negative things? I mean, throwing girls at your brother while he's with Laney? That's pretty low."

Roxy sucks in a slow breath while blinking back tears. "Ryder swore to me that if Laney ever took him back, he'd step away from the family. He meant my mother. He gets along fine with my dad and me. He said he'd cut out all family functions, anything that involved my mom." She runs her fingers through her magenta highlights before settling her eyes over mine. "I just want you and Ryder to be happy. You both deserve that. And nobody on this planet deserves to be treated the way my mother treated you. To say she can be judgmental is an understatement. In her own twisted way, she's just trying to protect my brother."

Baya reaches over and picks up my hand. "Laney, I'm so sorry. I can't imagine what it would be like if Bryson's mom said those things about me. But maybe you can sit down and talk to her? Maybe there's a way to work all this out. I'd hate to see you restart your relationship with him feeling like he needs to step out of his family."

"Have a civilized conversation with Rue Capwell?" I look to Roxy. "Is that even possible?"

"Anything's possible." Her eyes widen, and she looks decidedly like her brother. "I'll be there to mediate if you like."

"I'll gladly come and hold your hand," Baya offers.

I take a breath and mull it over. "Okay, but we should do it soon. I'd hate for Ryder to blow a hole in their relationship if it's not necessary."

"I'm sure it'll go well." Baya ventures on with her disillusioned innocence. "It's a necessary evil. Like pulling off a band aid."

Something tells me it will very much be necessary, but deep down I'm hoping it's not. I'd like nothing more than to start off on the right foot with Ryder, and cutting his mother out of his life doesn't exactly reek Norman

Rockwell—more like Norman Bates and we all know how that turned out.

Talking to Ryder's mother is going to be awkward. This won't be anything like ripping off a band aid—quite the opposite. This will be like taking a scalpel and reopening the wound.

It's going to hurt like hell.

I hope Ryder and I don't bleed out this time.

Ryder

Capwell Industries runs like a well-oiled machine, partly due to the fact my father is down on every dirty detail. He's completely hands-on when it comes to running his company and its many divisions, so much so that there's a high staff turnover from all the micromanagement taking place. And, in the same vein, my mother runs her life in a similar manner. She spends her days organizing charity functions for the local hospitals and universities, thus her appearance at the auction the other night. It's strange because she insisted I go. I had no idea Laney would be performing—that she would be auctioned off for the night no less. And I'm sure my mother was equally as surprised. I doubt she'd be so eager to get me "out of the house" if she knew it might land Laney in my bed for the night.

Hot damn that girl can light the sheets on fire. Still wish to God I had a "raincoat" lying around. Can't believe I let some sophomoric blunder take down the evening a notch. Not that it was ruined because every moment I spend with Laney is perfect, but it could have been elevated to a whole new level if I had the proper equipment to carry out the task at hand. I almost went for it. I came this close to playing God with both our futures and plunged into her, thrust after thrust, unstoppable. I'm glad I didn't though. Not that I don't want kids with Laney someday because I do. I want the whole happily ever after package, and if that means investing in a minivan and a never-ending supply of diapers so be it. With Laney by my side life is going to fade from a black and white world to a brilliant Technicolor surprise.

"What's up?" A hard slap lands over my shoulder, and I turn to find Bryson with a goofy grin on his face. "Heard you swept Sawyer off her feet last night."

"Good news travels fast." I nod him into my office, and he follows.

"Laney sort of left Baya holding the bag—her bag to be exact. So"—he connects his fingers at the tips as we take a seat—"speaking of bags, you bag anything last night? Anyone?"

"You're subtle." I open my laptop before relaxing into my chair. "Does 'sort of' count?"

"Sort of?" He looks amused then it quickly morphs into something shy of pity. "Bummer."

"No, definitely not a bummer. We held strong and put our bodies to good use. It's not that I couldn't, it's that I didn't have the proper equipment to wage war." I nod into him. "No battle helmet."

"Dude." Bryson pulls his wallet from the back of his jeans, and it looks as if he's literally pulling it out of his ass. "Make love not war and all that good shit." He flings a couple of foil packets my way.

"Thanks." I snap them up like they're Halloween candy. "I didn't know you were packing."

"Yeah, well, you never know when you're going to shoot a few off. Baya keeps me on my toes. You should get one of those industrial sized boxes," he teases. "The way you and Sawyer used to look at each other, you're going to need it."

"Duly noted, and we will most definitely need it."

Bryson nods into me. His expression grows somber, and I think I know where this is headed.

"So are things going to be different this time around?" The smile slips right off his face. He's gone from a dick-sock wielding buddy to Laney's over protective big bro in one easy bound.

"I'd never hurt her."

"I never said you would. How about your family? You think anyone might try to put her heart in the blender and serve it up with some mint leaves on the side?"

I nod, completely transfixed on some invisible horizon behind him.

"I'll talk to my mother. But I don't think I should wait for the first sign of bullshit to protect Laney. I'm afraid I need to cut my mom out of my life for a while. Maybe for good." I shake my head at the idea. "I hate it. But last time she went too far, and Laney left me. I can't go through that again, not for twelve seconds let alone twelve months."

"Let her know how you feel. Make sure she realizes how serious you are. I know your mom, Ryder. She's going to change her tune about Laney if it means losing you."

I blow out a breath and thread my hands behind my neck. "You're right. She means well, but she's toxic as hell when it comes to my love life. I think I'll stop by her office and have a little talk."

"You need some moral support?"

"Nope." I hold up the twin foil packets. "You did your good deed for today."

"Rock on, man." He leans over and throws a knuckle bump my way. "Guard Laney's heart. She's a sweet girl. She deserves to be happy, and so do you."

"Will do, and thank you. It's nice to see you smiling these days, too."

"I'm just glad Baya's safe. Any news about the trial?"

"None that I know of." My cousin Aubree was arrested last month for trying to kill Baya, and, apparently, there's strong evidence that suggests she did kill Stephanie Jones, a girl we grew up with. Bryson and Steph were together for a while, right up until she died. I can't imagine what it must have been like to go through something like that. And I never want to find out. I'd never say it to Bryson, but losing Laney for a year was enough to do me in. I still don't know how he catches his breath in the morning. I'm glad he found Baya to quell the pain.

"Let me know how things work out with your mom." He gets up and heads out the door. "We should take the girls out to dinner sometime. I think Baya and Laney would like that."

"I'd like that, too."

He takes off, and I shake my head with a goofy grin plastered to my face. I've gone from isolating myself at home to double dating—from romancing Rosie Palm to sleeping with Laney Sawyer.

I pinch the glorified love gloves between my fingers.

Soon Laney and I will commence our relationship in the best way possible, and, if last night was any indication of how incredible things are going to be, I'm betting I'll need two industrial-sized boxes to make it through this week alone.

Laney and I are together again, and nothing or nobody can tear us apart.

ಬಂಡ

That night I attended the show that the drama department put on and sat front and center. My mother had called earlier and invited me to dinner, but I took a rain check. She asked where I was off to so I told her. She responded with one word. *Wow.* I got the feeling it wasn't a good wow, so I didn't push it. I'm assuming it was more of a wow we're revisiting bad habits. She actually called Laney a bad habit to my face, last year, a few weeks before it all went down, and I let it slide because she's my mother.

I shake my head at the thought as I make my way to her office under a gloomy afternoon sky.

Laney and I ended up hanging out at her dorm after the show, and I spent the night holding her. One of Laney's roommates was home, so we decided to hold off in the pleasure department until tonight. But in a few hours, after her show, she'll be all mine. She says she'll pack a bag and spend winter break at the penthouse with me, and I cannot fucking wait. I'll gladly shuttle her to Whitney Briggs as needed. I'd shuttle her to Alaska and back if she wanted me to.

But right now I'm taking on the task of speaking with my mother. Her office is just across the street from Capwell Industries, so I head over and ride the elevator up, rehearsing what I'm going to say like some douchebag. I know she's going to be hurt. That she's going to feel threatened. I'm her only son, and she doesn't want to lose me. She's said, time and time again, that she only wants the best for me. Why in the hell can't she see that Laney is the best?

I step out onto her floor and make my way over to the Capwell Philanthropic offices, fully excepting to see Meg seated behind the big mahogany desk as I walk in but thankfully don't. She's abandoned her post for the moment. Probably drowning her sorrows now that she knows Laney and I are back together. Maybe she'll finally call off her stalker-like tendencies. I'd laugh it off, but she was close with Aubree, and come to find out, stalker-like tendencies were her specialty.

I walk over in the direction of my mother's office, and the sound of polite female laughter lights up the hall. Great. I'm sure my mother will invite Meg to sit in on our private conversation, no matter how hard I try to get rid of her. I catch the reflection of my mother's office from the mirrored hall and pause when I see them—Roxy, Baya and Laney, all three with bright red Santa hats on.

Holy shit. They beat me to it.

Laney didn't mention a meet and greet with my mother last night, and Roxy hasn't said anything. Maybe this doesn't have anything to do with me?

"Little Laney," Mom coos, talking down to the woman I love. It makes me sick to my stomach just hearing it. "If I've ever made you feel the slightest bit uncomfortable I do apologize. And I have nothing but the upmost respect for your mother, raising two daughters on her own after her husband so rudely walked out on her."

Rudely?

Shit.

Mom wags a finger. "I'm telling you, I should never have stayed true to my grandmother's century old eggnog recipe last year. It called for just a splash of rum, but I'm pretty sure I dumped in half the bottle. I swear I have no recollection of any of these things you've accused me of. It must have been the alcohol talking. Let me make this up to you. I'm having a dinner party tonight. I'd like to invite you all." She extends her hands to the three of them. "Bring dates, bring friends. I think this will be a great way to start things off in the right direction."

Roxy stands and lunges at Mom with a hug. The love fest begins, so I back the hell down the hall and out the building before they can spot me. It looks like I may not have to cut my mother out of my life after all.

My phone buzzes with a text. It's Laney. It's so nice to see her name light up my screen after one long year. Water finally comes to the desert.

Where are you?

Just getting ready to step back into my office. No lie, just stepped into the elevator.

I have a couple hours before the show. You mind if I stop by?

Come as quick as you can.

And with any luck she'll do just that.

5

With Bells On

Laney

The Capwell Industries building stands erect as a cosmopolitan symbol among the far more meager structures in the downtown district. The long, mirrored architecture curves at the top, giving it a phallic appeal as it spears into the sky. I soak it all in before stepping across the street to visit Ryder for the afternoon. It's as if with every step I take the relationship we're renewing becomes that much more official. It's strange to practically have Rue's blessing. I'm not sure I'm buying that "alcohol talking" excuse, but if that's the copout she's willing to use, I'm fine with it so long as it doesn't happen again.

"Wait for me!" Baya latches onto my arm. We're still wearing our matching Santa hats with bells attached to the giant fur ball, so we've quite literally jingled all the way here. Baya turns to Roxy. "Why don't you head back to campus? I'll catch a ride with Bryson."

"Will do." Roxy tugs at my sweater, splicing my attention for a moment. "So, what do you think? It sounds like she was genuine."

Rue's face flashes before my eyes. Somehow Rue and genuine don't seem to go hand in hand.

"Yeah—oh yeah." I think genuine is stretching it a little too far, but I'm not going there. "For sure she extended the olive branch, and I really appreciate it."

"So you'll be there tonight?" Roxy dips her knees when she says it as if she's pleading.

"Of course, I'm going to be there tonight—right after the show. It's the final performance before Christmas, and I'll even ditch the after-party just to make the effort. I really want things to go smoothly with your brother and me. I think this is a great start. And, I want your mom to like me." I blink back unexpected tears. "To be honest, up until today that wasn't all that important to me, but I really feel like you and Ryder are my family, and I'd like for your mother and me to feel the same one day, too."

"You will." She collapses her arms around me. "See you guys tonight!" She skips off to the parking lot, content in her delusions. Maybe I'm the one lost in my delusions? And negative ones at that. I *should* try harder, and if Rue is willing to meet me halfway, I'd better make the effort, too. But I can't shake this feeling she was just putting on an act because Roxy was there.

"What do you think?" I ask Baya as we cross the street.

"I don't know." She shakes out her long, dark tresses. "I think she said all the right words—smiled when it was required of her. She even threw in a joke at the expense of Whitney Briggs's rival." She shrugs as we walk into the polished building.

A two-story waterfall sits in the center of the foyer, and it takes my breath away for a moment. I forgot how beautiful this place is—how beautiful a lot of things are.

Baya scoots in close. "I say show up tonight and hope for the best." We step into the elevator and it entombs us with its quiet hush. "But just between you, me, and these four walls, I'd watch my back, Laney. Isn't she Aubree's blood relation? I doubt the apple falls far from the tree."

"Funny, she used that exact same analogy about me and my mother last year." I leave out the detail of my mother marrying for money when I was younger. About how her husband went into a coma and she was out spending his hard-earned cash when they finally pulled the plug. Word got around the hospital that she turned down the staff's offer to be there during those final moments when he left this planet. She opted to try on shoes and told the hospital to call her when he was done—like he was a fucking turkey. I still get pretty steamed over the fact my mother was a bona fide gold digger but having my dad walk out on her put her in a tailspin. Anyway—Baya and I step out into the advertising department, and I drop her off at Bryson's cubicle while I make my way over to Ryder's office.

The entire area has a black and white motif with mirrors strategically placed to make the space look even more expansive. My heart hammers in my chest as I take it all in. A cold sweat breaks out over me all at once. It's ridiculous for me to feel this way. I used to work right here in this building, on this floor. These are my old stomping grounds.

I glance over at the black lacquered desk I used to call my own. I was Ryder's personal secretary once upon a time. But after things ended badly I never came back. Lucky for me, Bryson let me work at the Black Bear, and the rest is waitressing history. I wonder if I'd want my old job back if Ryder made the offer? I remember each and every one of those stolen moments we shared in his office. God knows I've played them on a loop while snuggling up with my, "mini Ryder" after the split.

I give a gentle knock to his office door.

Hopefully we'll create a brand new memory this afternoon, and lucky for me because the real deal doesn't require a single AA battery.

"Come in." The baritone of his voice vibrates through the wood.

I step inside and close the door behind me, quiet as a whisper.

A breath gets caught in my throat at the sight of him as he rises from his desk. He's gorgeous as all hell in his sharp navy suit, his gold tie with crimson threads that pick up the light. His thick ebony hair is slicked back like the feathers of a raven. Those royal blue eyes light up the otherwise monochromatic room. He gives the slightest impression of a smile as his eyes glaze over with lust. His lids hood low while his chest rises and falls at an animated pace.

"What brings you to this side of town?" he asks as his dimples hedge in and out like shadows.

"You." I speed my way over, and he meets me at the edge of his desk. "Always you." I land my lips over his, and Ryder takes the initiative, spearing me lovingly with his tongue. He tastes fresh and minty as if he just rinsed with mouthwash, and it invites me to linger right there for another few minutes.

"Just me?" He peppers my face with kisses.

"I had a meeting with some friends."

"Sounds nice." He pulls back with a careful smile. "Do I know any of these friends?"

"Baya, Roxy"—I sigh—"your mother."

His dimples flex. "How did it go?"

I take in his warm cologne, and my panties melt to nothing. I still can't believe I'm standing here, in his office, with his heated hands secured over my hips. It all feels like a dream—the best dream.

"It went"—I clasp my fingers around his tie and pull him in—"really, really well." I land another boiling kiss over him. *God* I love Ryder's lips. It's like falling into a cloud, then his mouth opens, and you find that an entire supernova waits for you. I bump my tongue over his teeth before pulling away. "She invited us over to a dinner party she's having tonight, and I said I'd love to come after the show." I bounce my shoulders. "What do you think?"

He lets out a breath as if he's been holding it for weeks. "I think that's great. Are you sure you're okay with it?"

"I'm fine. I was able to share how I felt, and she apologized. And now we can kick-start our relationship with both our families intact. It's going to be great, Ryder."

"Good." He melts those lips over my mouth before tracking up to my ear. "Because I never want to see you get hurt again." He pulls back, and a pinch of grief sweeps over his features. "There's one more thing we need to discuss, but I don't think we need to go there right now." He tugs on the lip of my jeans. "Lose the clothes. Keep the hat." He flicks the ball dangling near my ear, and the bell goes off. "I'm about to make your wish come true."

"What wish is that?" I haven't a clue, but whatever the hell it is, it's safe to say I'm on board.

"You said you wanted to come after the show." He runs his tongue over the rim of my ear, and my skin lights up in a trail of prickles. "I'm going to make sure you come before and after. Consider it an early Christmas gift from my tongue to your—"

"Whoa, cowboy." I cut him off with a laugh caught in my throat.

Ryder zips across the room and locks the door. He sweeps the curtains closed, turning the oversized office into a virtual tunnel of darkness, or, more to the point, tunnel of love.

I jump out of my jeans and boots and peel off my sweater, leaving my red lace bra and underwear. Ryder and his prying eyes were exactly what I had in mind when I dressed myself this morning.

He swoops in from behind and lands a searing kiss just shy of my temple. I can feel his hard-on pressing against my bottom, and I reach back and run my fingers over the length of it.

"Since we're exchanging gifts a little early..." I purr, spinning in his arms. "I have something that I think *you* might like."

"I'm liking *you*." His lips run up and down my neck, leaving his silky suit pressed against my bare skin. "You're all the gift I need, Laney." He slips his fingers in my panties, and they voluntarily fall to the floor. "I'm the luckiest bastard alive. The only thing I want is my body in you."

I pull off his coat and work the buttons on his shirt.

"Well then"—I slip his belt off, nice and slow, never losing contact with his glowing eyes—"that fits right into my gift."

Ryder hoists me up onto his desk, and I knock over a glass of water—about a dozen objects go flying in every direction, and the intercom beeps for our attention. He brings his hand down over it before clearing the papers off the surface with a sweep of his arm.

"Is this where you're going to have me?" I land my legs on either side of him, trying not to wince as my skin adheres to the icy glass laid over his desk.

"This is just the beginning." His chest rattles over mine with a dark laugh. "I'm going to have you everywhere." He dots a kiss to my lips. "In every single way."

I run my fingers down his chiseled abs and a breath gets caught in my throat. "Ryder Capwell, you have been working out like a prisoner this past year, and you can't deny it because, believe you me, it shows." I wanted to say that to him the other night. I wanted to say a lot of things the other night, but whiskey and my stubborn ego prevented me from doing so.

I rake his shirt open, and my hands meander further south. There's a bulge in his boxers that borders on obscene, and it brings a smile to my face.

"I see my gift is waiting to be unwrapped." I work on his button before plunging his pants and boxers down past his thighs, and his most enthusiastic body part springs out and says, *hi there!*

He opens his desk an inch and pulls out a small gold packet.

"What's this?" For a second my heart lurches because somewhere in the distal part of my mind I thought it might be a ring. I can't even imagine relaying this story to our friends and relatives. *So how did he propose*, they'd ask, and I'd reply, *with a boner and a smile! Why, every part of his body was anxious to have me!* I relax when I see it's just a condom. "Is there rain in the forecast?" I'm not sure how we started calling them raincoats, but I like that we did. I like that we have an entire intimate world that only we're a part of.

"Oh, honey, it's going to pour." Ryder pulls me in by the back of the neck. He comes at me with hungry, anxious kisses. I wrap my legs around his waist as he lays his full weight over me for a moment. He props up on his elbows and traces out my lips with his tongue. His hand glides down to my thigh before he slips a finger deep inside me, and I moan with approval.

"*Ryder.*" I reach down and guide him to that special place that's been burning to have him ever since that night so long ago. It's been a whole year of no action, well, not by a real live human at least. I'm pretty sure sex toys don't count. In fact, if you want to get technical, I'm pretty sure I've renewed my virgin standing. "Hey, you know what I just thought of?"

"Mmm?" He tears open the foil packet with his teeth.

"I'm sort of a virgin again. So you know what that means right?"

His dimples flex in amusement. "That I'm an even luckier bastard than I suspected?"

"And that I'm going to bleed out all over your desk," I tease. When Ryder and I first had sex I was, what I like to call, *extra virgin*. My dorm sheets looked like a massacre just took place, and Ryder was more than a little panicked when we were through. I may or may not have led him to believe he punctured my uterus, and, even though it's impossible to do so, I really had him going.

He pushes a dull laugh into my ear. "No blood please—now, blood curdling *screams* that's another story."

"You do like me vocal, don't you?" I bring the tip of him into me, and he sucks in a quick breath through his teeth as if he touched a flame.

"You okay?"

"You feel *so* fucking fantastic." He lets out a groan as if he were in pain. "Trust me, I'd love to bury myself in you without anything on—that's pretty big on my bucket list—lots of naked-penis sex."

My chest bubbles with a laugh. I brush my finger over his brow. Ryder has the most amazing eyebrows, thick and dark like the wings of a majestic bird in flight.

"God, you're hot." I bite down over a smile. "But you know that, don't you?"

He leans up and pulls the raincoat out of its tiny foil home, and I pluck it from him and pitch it over my shoulder.

"What did you do that for?" He looks vexingly perplexed, and it only makes me want him more.

I pull him in by the shirt until he's tucked in close.

"I want you in me, sans the raincoat," I whisper. "Right now it's all about your big naked penis. It's my gift to you."

He laughs into my mouth before swiping his tongue over mine.

"I think we should put off the family for another few years. But, lucky for you, I'm pretty well stocked." He reaches into his drawer and produces another one.

"Are you manufacturing them in your desk?" I tease as I snatch it from him and pitch it over my shoulder like I did the last one.

"Laney." He stretches up over me and searches the floor for the glorified water balloons. "We need those."

"No we don't." I take a breath. "Last year"—a lump the size of a Christmas ornament lodges in my throat—"I went on the pill. I trust you, Ryder. You're the only man I ever want to be with, and I haven't even thought about another person this last year except for you."

"Laney." He brushes the hair from my face sweetly. "I haven't thought of, or looked at, another person for the past twelve months."

"Are you trying to one-up me?"

His chest vibrates with a dull laugh. "No, but I want to make the point I'm all yours, and I'm clean."

"No acid rain?" Despite the crude and disturbing imagery it's really a lovely thought.

"Nope." He lands a careful kiss over my lips. "You can bottle it and drink it if you wanted."

"Okay, that was gross." I swat him over the arm. The only thing I want to bottle is his love for me. "How did we go from I'm ho, ho, ho happy to see you, to bloody desk tops and bottled sperm?"

"I think that's what makes us, *us*." His dimples flex, no smile. Ryder always knows the right answer.

"You know what else makes us, *us*?" I gently press him in by the small of his back. "You, deep inside me."

Ryder

I should really get a couch in here.

Laney writhes beneath me ready and willing to help me take the plunge of a lifetime, and all the while I feel bad for having her beautiful body sprawled out over my desk. It's got be cold—hell, it's covered with a sheet of glass so I know it is, and her back must be killing her, but Laney has never been one to complain.

She gurgles out a dark laugh and pulls me in by the tie. "Are you ready, cowboy?"

My lips twitch with a brief smile. Twice she's called me that. I might have to go out and get us a matching pair of boots and some spurs just to keep her in line. I lash my tongue over her neck while making my way to her sweet, perfect ear and whisper, "A big storm's coming from my region. Are *you* ready?"

Laney lets out a groan as I work my fingers over her perfect tits. Her nipples harden beneath me, and I pinch her bra down until she springs right out of it.

"I was sort of hoping a big earthquake would strike my neck of the woods soon," she whispers into my mouth.

"That's funny, I was just about to arrange for multiple tremors. You'd better brace yourself, I hear the big one's coming."

"Maybe you should hold me down and keep me safe?" She bats her lashes at me. "You know, pin me beneath you—that way I won't roll off the desk and hurt myself." Laney reaches down and circles the tip of my dick over her heated slick, and I let out a fierce groan that wrenches from deep inside me. I've fantasized about Laney Sawyer for years, and not one time did any of those fantasies involve a piece of latex dividing her body from mine. This is it, the real deal. I'm going to feel Laney's body from the inside for the very first time.

"It's okay"—she whispers directly into my ear, and a fire rips up my spine—"I want you to."

That's all the green light I need. My body plunges into hers, slow and careful.

"Oh shit," I give it as a heated charge right over her lips. "You're so fucking tight," I pant. She wasn't kidding. She's a bona fide virgin again, and it's a slice of Heaven.

I can *feel* her. My eyes spring wide as I take in the slick sensation that I've been deprived of hundreds of times before. Her body conforms to mine like an oven-heated glove, and my dick straightens like a pool stick.

"You feel incredible." She rubs her lips over my ear in a heated rush as I give a pronounced thrust into her.

"*You* feel incredible." I sweep kisses over her features, quick and pressured. "You're the best damn gift. I'm glad you're in my life. This is Christmas right here." I land my lips over her forehead a moment before plunging into her the way I want. "You're going to come for me." I reach down and find her with my finger, easing my movements in order to create small circles over that tender part of her.

Laney lets out a groan that has the ability to rattle the windows.

"*Ryder.*"

I lift her tit into my mouth and suck down hard until she's clawing at my back. I launch an assault on her poor body that has her panting, and moaning, and creating those cute noises with her vocal cords that make me certifiably insane.

"Shit." I'm right there, and I don't think I can hold it for another second. I work my fingers over her fast and furious and land a soft pinch over her folds until Laney loses it, and so do I.

I come for weeks, for years, pouring out all of my desire for the only woman I love, right into her beautiful body.

Her heart knocks against my chest like it's begging to be let in, and I give a little smile right over her lips.

"I love you," she pants into my ear.

"I love you, too, Laney."

Laney holds me down by the back of my neck and lounges her tongue in my mouth like it's setting up shop, ready to take up residence for years.

A dull clapping noise comes from the north end of the desk, and Laney and I both look over at the same time.

An orange light blinks on and off and, "Holy fuck." I slap at it until the damn intercom shuts off. It flies off the desk, and I pull at the wires until it loosens from the plug.

Crap.

Laney touches her hand over her mouth. "You think they heard?"

"Every damn thing." I hold back the laugh already brewing in my chest. "At least they were polite enough to applaud our efforts."

"Not bad for our first live performance." Laney bites down over my lower lip.

"First and last." I dot each of her lids with a kiss. "I like the idea of it being a private show."

"Personal invite only." She runs her hands over my bare ass and gives a squeeze.

I gaze down at her, admiring the glow that's rising to her cheeks. "Did you pack your bags?"

She nods with her lips pressed tight. "We can put them in your trunk before the show, that way we can go straight to your place after your mom's."

My stomach grinds for a moment. "That's a great plan." Not so much the part about going to my mother's. I'm not too sold on the idea she'll mind her P's and Q's. My mother isn't one to go down quietly. If she's got a beef with someone she pretty much likes to hold onto it, and God knows she has a beef with Laney over just about everything.

Last Christmas Eve comes to mind, and I'm quick to push it away. Going back to that night is like stepping in front of an oncoming train, time and time again, and expecting different results. It doesn't do any good. But I know Laney and I should go there at least one more time just to make sure we've sealed that door shut tight. Damn Meg—and my mother—for everything that went down.

I rub my eyes for a moment as I lie next to Laney on the unforgivably cold, hard desk.

"*Aww*," she coos, kissing the side of my face with a tenderness I don't remember ever seeing from her before. "Do you need a little nap?" She wraps her arm over my waist, and I cinch her in close.

"You know what I need?" I bury a kiss in her neck. She's adjusted her bra back into position, and her skin glows from under the red lace. Her Santa hat is still firmly in place, and she looks adorable as hell. "I need a couch in here so we can do this all the fucking time."

She bubbles out a laugh.

"You're lewd and crude, you know that? And I wholeheartedly agree about the couch. In fact, we should shop for it together—test it out, right there on the showroom."

"Sounds like a repeat performance might be necessary."

"We can practice later tonight."

"Every night," I counter.

"Every single night." Her lips fall over mine. Laney and I love each other with our mouths fused together until the sun goes down.

This is shaping up to be the best damn Christmas ever.

₨₩

Later that night, Laney shines on stage. Her performance is stunning, as is Laney, herself. Once it's through, I jump to my feet and clap the loudest and longest. The stage may be filled with the entire ensemble, but I can't take my eyes off the girl who stole my heart. Her hair is ratted out, her dress is torn and disheveled, and she's covered with soot from head to toe, but, God almighty, Laney Sawyer outshines every person in this room.

Afterwards, I wait outside the theater with a bouquet of two-dozen bright red roses. My trunk is already locked and loaded with her things, and I can't wait to spend the rest of winter break with her in my penthouse—with me— right where she belongs. And, if I get my way, she'll be a permanent resident.

"Hey!" She squeals as she treks over in her killer high heels, her down to there and up to here little black dress. Her hair is smoothed out in perfect waves, and there's not a trace of soot over her porcelain features.

"These are for you." I hold out the flowers as she jumps into my arms.

"They're beautiful."

I lean back and take her in. "Wow." It's the only word that can accurately describe how sublime she looks right now.

"Wow, yourself." She pulls me in by the collar. "Have I ever told you how much I love you in a suit?"

A lazy smile slopes up my cheek. "Have I ever told you how much I love you naked in my bed?"

"Mmm," she purrs into me with kiss. "By the way, as much as I do love you in a monkey suit, I love your naked penis a whole lot better. That felt incredible this afternoon."

"That did feel incredible." I pull her in and grind my hips over hers so she gets the full effect of the attention my lower half so desperately wants to give her. "And is the naked penis a thing now?"

"Hell *yes*." A tiny dimple goes off in her cheek. I swear, Laney gets cuter by the minute. "I think it's always been a thing. Your thing." She reaches down and rubs her hand over me. "And now it's sort of my thing, too."

I narrow my gaze into hers while bringing my hands up to her nipples and rubbing my thumbs over them. "I like sharing things with you."

"What's mine is yours." She laughs into her kiss. "Let's get to your parent's house so we can wrap this night up. I'm already looking forward to the big finish starring the Big N.P." She gives my crotch a gentle squeeze.

I huff a laugh. "I won't lie, my ego likes that you put the word 'big' in front of N.P." Laney's dirty mouth coupled with her wit and charm are what drew me to her in the first place.

"Nice touch right?"

"It's all you."

She bubbles with a laugh. "I'm always looking for a classy move to impress you." Laney gives a playful wink because I happen to know she thinks the word "classy" is a joke.

"I like the sound of that." I pull her in by the waist as we make our way through the parking lot. "The Big N.P. can't wait to hook up with your Red River Valley."

"*Eww* and no to the not-so-cute moniker." She swats me over the arm with her flowers. "How about the Door of Life?"

"Too formal."

"Grandest Canyon?"

"I think we've safely determined you're more of a tight little ravine kind of a girl." I plant a kiss over her forehead. "How about, Slice of Heaven?"

"*Aww.* I love that." She tightens her grip around my waist.

"Just a few more hours, and I'll be in paradise."

"Me too, Ryder." She leans her head on my shoulder, and the roses crush between us. "I'm always in paradise with you."

ဆၢၪ

My mother has a habit of going all out for the holidays. She puts most public displays to shame with her extensive and thorough ninja decorating skills. Of course, she didn't lift a finger to actually deck the halls. She has a small army of staffers who live to grace the house with miles of garland, lights, enough trees to qualify it as the Capwell forest, and, of course, a thousand little knickknacks anywhere and everywhere you'd think to look in the event you forgot it was Christmas. Green, red, silver, and gold—it's all here, present and accounted for, along with miles and miles of garland.

We bypass the oversized nativity on the lawn, with the manger still empty, waiting for the little king to make his debut tomorrow at midnight.

"You ready?" I nod at the cut glass doors. Even from this vantage point we can see a room full of people, the laughter of the crowd echoes right through the walls.

"I'm more than ready," she assures, pulling me forward as if she were looking to get this over with, and, truth be told, I couldn't blame her because so am I. The next stop after this is Heaven, and I can't wait to plunge inside those pearly gates.

I pull her in for one last embrace before we descend the gates of, for a lack of a better word, hell.

"Let's do it." I don't bother knocking, we just head on in, and the sound of holiday music and laughter goes up several octaves. The scent of fresh cut pine and cinnamon infiltrate the air, and the hint of something delicious and far more packed with protein is layered just beneath that—prime rib. "You want to grab a bite?" I'm already pulling her toward the buffet.

"I'm not that hungry." She looks around at the crowd, and you can practically see the nerves jumping in her eyes. Figures. Laney can perform to a crowd of thousands, and yet the thought of being in a room with my mother has her crawling out of her skin. "Maybe we should say hi to your mom first?"

"You always were the smart one."

"Says the one who runs a multi-billion dollar company." She gives my hand a squeeze.

"Not quite, but someday." It's true. I've been grinding the gears down at the farm since middle school, and I know damn well how to make Capwell Inc. run like a fuel-efficient machine. In addition to that, I've bought and traded enough stocks and assets over this last year alone to create a nice financial cushion for Laney and me. A smile tugs at my lips at the thought of a future with Laney. I'm already living the dream.

We spot my mother over by the fireplace with a group of investors. I recognize them from a meeting the other day. Dad is still in Japan, but he'll be home tomorrow night, so Mom is flying solo this evening. She looks calm, cool, and collected. She has her fingers coiled around a glass of wine and a wide painted smile stretching across her face. It looks like a good time to catch her.

The group she's with shares a laugh before disbanding, and we come up on her quick before she's pulled away by the crowd.

"Look who decided to show up?" Her eyes expand as she gives a toothy smile, and I can't for the life of me figure out if she's thrilled or pissed. You'd think I would have decoded my mother's many moods by now, but I'm not even close. Not sure I want to be.

"It's nice to see you, too," I chime in.

"Great party." Laney marvels at the guests a moment. "And the decorations! Your home is to die for."

"It is a stunner." She pulls back and examines Laney from head to toe. "And look at you."

I wrap my arm around Laney and wait for my mother to follow her observatory remark with something nice, but it doesn't come. I think we both know that's as close as my mother gets to doling out a compliment, she tiptoes to the border and ventures no further.

"Oh, the chancellor from the auxiliary league is making her way to the door. I'll catch up with you two later." She zips off to tend to her guests, and I breathe a sigh of relief.

"That went well." Laney glances at the ceiling as if she were considering it. Come to think of it, she was probably posing a question.

"How about you and me head over to that buffet now?" I nip at her earlobe, and she bucks and shudders beneath me. It's like the public version of an orgasm—one I don't mind gifting her right here under my mother's uptight roof. These are the exact things I've missed this past year. The way her body responds to mine, her cute sighs, the sweet way she rubs my back when we're in public. I'm addicted to it all.

"Why don't you go ahead? I see Baya and Roxy outside, and I want to say hello."

"You bet." I crash my lips to hers for a moment. "I'll be out in a sec."

She drifts off with a wave, and I make a beeline toward the food. It's a holiday spread that only my mother's careful culinary supervision can provide. I must say, I'm damn glad Laney and Mom have worked things out. As much as I'd miss my mother, I'd miss her five-star catered events as well. I suppose that sounds cruel, but the food has been known to offer more comfort and support than the woman herself. Nevertheless my stomach lives to eat another Capwell-catered meal.

"Hey, good looking." A female voice sings to my right, followed by a nudge to the shoulder.

I glance down to find Meg with her eyes rotating in her skull, her lipstick smeared.

"You okay?" Shit. This is exactly how it went down last year, but this time I'm not falling for anybody's party tricks. If Meg wants to use and abuse her liver, it's entirely up to her. She can fall flat on her face, and I'll be the first to find someone to help her, but it won't be me.

"I'm better now." She sticks to my side like we're glued at the hip, and my body temperature spikes because I'm terrified Laney will walk in and see the display.

"Good." I move away as I reach for a plate.

"Rumor has it you and Laney are at it again."

At it again? She makes it sound like a fistfight.

"Yup. Some rumors are true. We're at a lot of things again." Take the hint and leave. I scoop dish after dish onto my plate, and yet Meg has my appetite waning. If she keeps this up, I'll miss out on a great dinner.

"So this is something you want?" She leans against the counter and a ladle of rice rockets in the air, spraying the two of us with hundreds of sticky grains.

"Hold your fire." I dust myself off, and she takes the opportunity to molest the hell out of my chest. I can smell the hint of liquor on her breath, and you don't need to be a genius to know where this is headed.

"I'm so sorry!" She pants through a laugh. "It's like some crazy wedding omen."

Crazy being the operative word.

"I've got this," I say as I back the hell away. "And, yes, when the time is right Laney and I will marry." There. Done. I set down my food and turn to head outside.

"You can't marry, Laney. We haven't done this—" She spins me around by the back of the neck and pushes her lips to mine.

6

Deck the Halls and Maybe Meg

Laney

Roxy is laughing her ass off while Baya spells out in nauseating detail what went down at the office today.

"The intercom!" Roxy belts it out with a scream. "That's classic! I bet Ryder gets a lot more respect around the office from now on." She digs her fingers into her eyes as she wipes away the tears.

"I do what I can to help."

Baya breaks out into slow moans, "*Oh Ryder—Oh shit, Laney*, and *dear God, your penis is naked!*"

"I did not say that." I avert my gaze for a moment at Bryson who thankfully is seemingly distracted by something in the house. "And that's not how it went at all."

"Well, maybe next time you can leave the door wide open so we can get a visual." Baya pulls Bryson in close as they share a laugh.

Very funny.

"You can sell tickets!" Roxy chortles. "I bet that would really help out the drama department."

Sell tickets. I shake my head. But it's all in fun, and, after all, Ryder and I sort of set ourselves up for this. I have a feeling he'll be getting rid of the intercom sooner than later. At the very least, a nice fluffy couch will soon make its appearance. If I had the cash, I'd pony up for one myself.

Baya and Roxy settle down—actually they stop in their tracks, and now the three of them are staring at the house with their faces as white as ghosts.

"What?" I go to spin around, and Roxy catches me, preventing me from doing so. "I'm going to find out, so you might as well let me see."

God, what if Ryder is planning some spectacular proposal, and he's about to bring out the ring on a silver platter with fireworks and a marching band and an entire cheerleading squad. Wait—nix the cheerleaders. The only one allowed to be remotely cute and sexy in the engagement processional is me. My fantasy. My rules.

Roxy loosens her grasp and shoots a dirty look behind me.

I turn to find Ryder barreling in this direction, and practically tackle him, ready to say yes, when I spot bright red lipstick smeared over his mouth. Crap. It looks like someone beat me to the kissing portion of my daydream.

I run my finger through the kiss-print and hold it up for him to see. "I think pink is more your color. What's this about?"

"Meg." He grunts her name out like a curse as he wipes his mouth down with the back of his hand.

"You care to explain?" My heart thumps unnaturally, and I feel sick to my stomach. Good thing I skipped dinner, or we'd be staring at my regurgitated meal all over Ryder's patent leather shoes.

"I wish I could." He shakes his head. "One minute I'm scooping out the stroganoff, and the next thing I know, she's trying to play tonsil hockey."

"Tonsil hockey?" I suck in a never-ending breath. "Those are *my* fucking tonsils." I pivot on my heels and make a dash for the house. I traverse bodies and a bevy of annoying faux gifts that Rue has stacked around the mansion to give it that we-believe-in-holiday-excess appeal. Honest to God, the way that woman spends money you'd think it were her sole responsibility to kick-start the economy. And who the hell says, *Look at you!* And doesn't follow it up with something nice?

My anger ping pongs from her to Meg, and now I'm not sure either one is safe. God only knows what will happen to the one I see first.

There she is.

Meg.

She's huddled in the arms of some gold lame wearing socialite, and I'll be damned if it's not Rue herself.

"Well, look who's here?" I force a smile to expand and retract.

Meg cowers in Rue's arms with her lipstick smeared around her mouth like a clown. God, she even *looks* mental. She probably is, but I won't let that stop me from punching her in the throat. I'm not above going street on her, right here, in front of all of Rue's high society fake friends.

Meg sneers while nestled in Rue's gorilla-like embrace.

Anger courses through me like rocket fuel. My adrenaline percolates like a pot with the lid ready to dance right off.

"Who the hell do you think you are?" I give a hard shove into her chest, and Ryder comes up from behind and pulls me back. "No." I push him away as Roxy pops up beside him. Baya and Bryson wisely stand to the side. "I get to say to my piece." I yank Meg in by her Peter Pan collar. And who the hell wears a Peter Pan collar? I swear the last time I saw one was in a picture of my mother while I was still swimming in her belly. "Nineteen ninety-one called, and it wants its maternity wear back."

"What?" Both she and Rue look stunned and confused.

"Okay, that was sort of ridiculous," Roxy says, trying to coax me away by snatching at my elbow.

"I'll think of something better at three in the morning"—I lean into Meg—"while I'm lying in Ryder's *arms*."

"Don't waste your time with her." Ryder tries to pluck me back. "Let's get out of here."

"No." Rue holds up a finger. "By all means say your piece, Laney. I'd hate for you to run off for another year and create an even bigger rift between my son and I." She glowers into me because we both know she'd like nothing more than for me to disappear for a lifetime.

"*Mom*," Ryder says the reprimand sweet enough, but it's too late. She's already opened the Pandora's box of yesteryear, and all of the ugly truths are flying around us, tangling in our hair like bats.

"Ryder and I are together again." I practically spit the words into Meg's snooty uptight, pinched nose, thin lipped, pale as plaster face. "Let me outline this for you. That means you may never plant your greasy red lips on him again. *And*, if you even so much as wink at him, I'll plant my fist in your jaw." I step in until we're nose to nose. "You have nice teeth, Meg. Don't go risking years of orthodontia in order to lure my boyfriend into your bed because it ain't happening bitch."

A loud collective gasp circles the room, and I'm only slightly horrified to see an entire herd of elderly people gathered around for the show, but walkers and wheelchairs be damned because this is one show that's about to go on.

Rue clears her throat. "Ryder if you would, please remove your friend from the premises." She speeds the words from the side of her lips. "She's causing a scene."

"I'll leave once I get an apology." I glare into Meg as she cowers behind Ryder's mother like she's some rabid girlfriend protection shield. Little does she know I'll take the both of them down if I have to, and every bit of me is committed to the effort.

"Apologize?" Rue snorts. "How about you apologize to my guests for ruining their night—to the geriatric foundation whose only outing this month was this very gathering. Please take your incredibly bad manners and leave. This is a *Christmas* party, Laney, not one of your mother's bar brawls."

My hand flies over her cheek so fast, I swear the thought to hit her never crossed my mind. It's like I was possessed or level headed, either or.

"Crap," I whimper, because, for one, assaulting the guest of honor is never a good thing and double crap because she just so happens to be my boyfriend's mother.

"Oh, Laney." Roxy wraps her arms around me tight as if I were already being hauled off to prison. God knows a bitch slap isn't your typical felony offence but something tells me Rue's legal team is more than capable of parlaying a death sentence out of it.

"Call the police," Rue whispers to the woman patting her cheek down with a napkin dipped in champagne. And as if it weren't bad enough to have bitch slapped my prospective future mother-in-law, half the guests are shaking their grey heads in my direction.

"Ryder." I turn to him, and he takes me in his arms.

"It's okay," he whispers. "You don't need to call the police." He informs the woman wearing head to toe rubies. I'm pretty sure those non-eco friendly gems she's sporting have cost at least a dozen people their lives. And there's no way in hell those diamonds bejeweling her neck are conflict free because if she's a friend of Rue's, she loves conflict. Each new day for the rich and infamous brings a fresh scoop of misery with a little conflict on the side. And here we are, with heaping piles of both. "We're out of here."

"*No*," Rue barks. She settles her narrowed gaze over me, and I can feel the hatred spewing from her like a tidal wave, but it's always been there. Today in the office with all that manufactured kindness, those unnatural grimaces she tried to pass off as smiles, those felt horrifically fake—but this, *this* feels downright genuine. "I demand an apology, to the both of us." She shoulders up to Meg, who she might actually care for more than her own daughter, but I wouldn't dare say it to Roxy.

"Don't apologize." Roxy stands beside me, defiant.

"Roseanna, keep your thoughts to yourself." Rue scowls at her openly. "This doesn't concern you." The fine lines around her eyes and mouth multiply, making her look a thousand years old and scary as hell.

Wow. It looks like someone's Botox just said fuck you.

"She's right," Ryder grunts. "This doesn't concern you, Roxy. It concerns *me*."

My adrenaline ticks up a notch, and suddenly I want nothing but for this to end.

I glance at Meg with her lipstick smeared—a sorrowful look on her face because she'll never have Ryder.

"I'm sorry I pushed you." There. "I mean it."

Meg makes a face and only ends up looking that much more demented.

I turn to Rue, Satan's own spawn. Okay, so that's probably a little harsh, but I defer to that whole adrenaline thing. I might have something nicer to call her in the morning, but somehow I doubt it.

"But *you*"—I start—"were very disrespectful to my mother. I am not apologizing." Accurate as hell, but nonetheless.

"I only call it like I see it." Rue sweeps over me as if she were dismissing the help.

"Well then, I'm going to call it like *I* see it."

Ryder sags a little because he knows this isn't going to end well.

"Go ahead," he whispers. "I want you to."

A new sense of resolve fills me. With Ryder on my side, I've already won. I'll have to reward the Big N.P. later with a treat of vaginal proportions, but I was already planning to do that anyway. Maybe we could involve chocolate somehow? But his bedroom is so damn nice it'd be a pity. Hey, we should totally go to one of those twenty-four hour convenience stores and invest in a tarp. Nothing says bring on the chocolate syrup like a ten-by-fourteen piece of waterproof poly.

"Well?" Rue barks, and I snap out of my chocolate-inspired stupor.

Here it goes. "I *did* hit you, but you were very inconsiderate." Honest to God, I swear that qualifies as an apology somewhere in this twisted world. "I can only take so much before I snap, and apparently tonight that line was my mother. She may not be perfect but she's not here to defend herself either, and I'm a big believer in saying things to people's faces. So the next time you decide to call me a whore, make sure I'm in the room to hear it. Or maybe you prefer your lackey to do your dirty work for you, which brings me to my next point—*Meg*. If you had a boyfriend, I could guarantee you I wouldn't throw myself at him at a Christmas party even if I were shitfaced off century old eggnog and desperate to get laid. You have no right to lock lips with anyone without their permission, and I doubt very much Ryder was a willing participant. Hands off, *bitch*. He's mine." That ought to get the point across. And, if it doesn't, I happen to be wearing my roach killing FMs courtesy of the Whitney Briggs drama department, and they look like they could slide nicely right up her ass.

"Is this what you want?" Rue tosses her hand in my direction while challenging Ryder with a guilt-riddled stare. "Someone who curses in the presence of the elderly—people of noble character?" She pans the grey-haired mafia, all of which happen to be scowling at me. "Someone who accosts your mother over words? The *truth* no less?" She shakes her head with a frown dripping down her lips. "This isn't the kind of wife your father and I envision for you. When you come to your senses, I'm sure someone with grace and good character will be waiting for you." She wraps her arm around Meg. "Sow your oats quickly, Ryder. This is disheartening for everyone involved."

A loud clatter comes from the entry as an entire swarm of Hollow Brook's finest pour into the overgrown house.

"Wait," Ryder roars it out and garners the attention of the entire room. "I'm not marrying Meg—not now or ever. And Laney is right." He jabs a finger in Meg's direction. "You can't dry hump me in public or in private"—he points over to his mother—"and you can't talk to the woman I love that way. I don't care how many five-star meals I miss, you won't see me coming around here anymore."

Five-star meals? He really is sacrificing big time.

Rue flicks her wrist. "She's left you once, she'll do it again."

"You should watch your back, Ryder." Meg pipes up and stuns just about everyone. Who knew she had hormones *and* a voice? And to think she's wielding them both like a weapon on the very same night. "Since we're on the topic of her mother, didn't she poison one of her many husbands for his money?"

Boy the rich really know how to take that whole "your mama" thing to an entirely new level.

I choke trying to get the words out. "My mother is *not* a murderer." And why the hell are we stuck on my poor mom anyway?

"No." Meg sharpens her eyes on me. "But maybe *you're* a gold digger."

I suck in a breath. Good God if the Hollow Brook P.D. weren't out in force tonight, I would have gladly clocked her.

Oh, what the hell.

I lunge in her direction, and a tall, navy suited officer catches me in the air like a pop fly. He kindly escorts me off the premises backward, with my heels dragging, my hands swinging into thin air. But it still feels pretty damn good because all the while Ryder is by my side.

Ryder

The officer dumps us off at the foot of the lawn before heading back into the house.

"Well, there's that." Roxy slaps her hands together as if she's wiping them clean in a symbolic, we've just taken our mother out with the trash, kind of way. "I'll get my things and take off. I think I'll make up a plate to go. Baya, Bryson, you in?"

"We'll pass." Baya shoots a dirty look into the party before reverting her attention to me. "Take care of Laney for me, and if I don't see you guys, merry Christmas." She pulls us both into a quick embrace, and I knuckle bump Bryson.

"Will do," I say. "Roxy," I call my sister over and give her a hug. "Do what you want. It's Christmas, and I know Dad is dying to get home to see you." I press a quick kiss over her cheek. "We'll get together and exchange gifts some other time."

"All right, but I'll be moving on the twenty-sixth, so maybe sometime later in the week."

"Where you going?" I'm mildly alarmed. I can't stand the thought of my entire family blowing apart and moving to the four corners of the globe, especially not Rox—we're close and I want to keep it that way.

"I'm moving in with a friend." She cuts a quick look to Baya and Bryson. "He's got an oven, and there's this big baking competition coming up with ten thousand dollars on the line and an internship at the Sticky Quicky—"

"*He*?" I'm stuck on go. Never mind the fact she just said the words *Sticky Quicky* in the same sentence. "No way."

"Relax." Bryson holds up a hand. "It's my old roommate. And Baya and I will be right next door. If Roxy so much as whimpers, I'll be on it."

Baya leans in. "Cole is her new roommate. He's my overprotective big brother. I promise you, she'll be safe." Baya wraps her arms around Bryson, and they both grin like a couple of loons.

That's all I want is for Laney and me to end this night happy as a couple of loons, so I opt not to fight my sister over the fact she's using some guy for confectionary purposes. Roxy is plenty beautiful. There's no doubt in my mind this moron is going to try something. I'm the one who will have to be on it. She can expect more than her fair share of visits from her own overprotective big bro.

"All right." I hug Roxy once again and so does Laney. "Good night."

Everyone says goodnight, and the girls scream merry Christmas until we're safely tucked in my car, and I speed us the hell out of there.

ಐಐಬ

Laney and I finally get to the penthouse, and I make a fire while she sits by the colorful, albeit seizure-inducing tree and admires it.

I land beside her and pull her beautiful body right into my lap. "It's midnight. Merry Christmas, baby." I plant a lingering kiss on her cheek. Technically it's Christmas Eve, but every day with Laney feels like Christmas.

"You know what I'm hoping to find in my stocking this year?" She twists into me until we're facing one another. "The Big N.P. and your face with a smile." There's a twinge of sadness in her eyes, and her lips quiver despite her attempt to make me laugh.

"Done and done." I land a wet kiss over her trembling lips.

"My mom invited us to spend Christmas Eve with her and my sister. You think you'll be up for that?"

"You kidding? Your mother loves me. I'll be there with bells on, literally if you want. She still loves me, right?"

Laney winces while measuring a slim distance between her thumb and forefinger. "But the best part is, she still likes you better than me." She pushes into me playfully as the smile melts off her face. "I feel selfish doing anything with my mother now."

"Don't." I try to stop her from going to any dark places. "Everything that happened tonight—it's over, and so is that part of our lives."

She closes her eyes and sighs. "I hate that I ruined your family."

"You didn't ruin anything."

"I overreacted."

"Not true. If some idiot were trying to manhandle you, I would have done a lot worse. Let's just say the stroganoff would have went flying. I would have involved dinner, dessert, dishes, *and* furniture. The entire swat team would have showed. If anything, I think you were a lady about the whole thing."

"Please don't let this kill the relationship with your mother. I feel terrible."

"She killed it. You didn't." I press a kiss over the top of her head. "I don't want you to feel bad. Maybe in the future, when she comes to her senses, we'll work things out, but, for now, I'm through with her. You're not some wild oat, Laney. You're the love of my life. You're the woman I want to spend every last breath with and there's not another soul on the planet who's going to get in the way. This is it, you and me. This is real. This is what I want." I take in a breath because I know where we need to go next, and I don't want to.

"Ryder." She moves her hands over my back and warms me. "You know I love you more than the universe and everything in it. I'd die to be with you. I *do* owe someone an apology tonight, and it's you." She glances down and picks up my hand. "Last year I was driven to the brink of insanity with all that Meg drama. And that night"—her back trembles as she fights the tears—"I couldn't take it anymore. I felt like you were choosing her. That I would never fully have you—that maybe I wasn't enough."

"You are *more* than enough." I pull her in close and bring her lips to mine for a moment. "I swear to you, I wasn't choosing her. I would never choose anyone over you, and, if I could go back in time, I'd do everything different." I rock her in my arms. "I'm the one who owes you an apology. Weeks before that night my mother tried everything to undermine our relationship, but I kept making excuses for her. Deep down I didn't want to believe she was capable, that she would be heartless enough not to care what I wanted—that she'd push off her own desires on me. That night, I held you in my arms until you fell asleep. I got a text from my mother. She said I needed to get to the house right away, that it was an emergency." My voice cracks because it was the last time I would hold Laney until just a few days ago. "I thought it had something to do with my dad. I just took off without thinking. When I got to the house she said Meg fell down the stairs—that she was fine but asked if I could take her home."

"That's what she wanted—you out of my bed and with Meg."

"And that's when you came." I drove Meg to her place. "She asked me to help her to bed, and I fell for it. Meg pulled off her dress. I swear I didn't do it." That's when Laney burst through the doors with a fire in her eyes.

"You had spent so much time rescuing her like some poor, feeble kitten stuck in a tree, I was sick and tired of it. Seeing her like that—naked. Seeing you with her in the same bedroom." She shakes her head. "That was the last straw. It was all I could take."

"I'm sorry. You were right about everything. I swear I'll never doubt you again." I press my lips to her hair. "I've always wondered, how did you know to come?"

"I got a text." Her pale eyes glitter with tears. "Meg said you were taking her to bed." She presses her lips tight and swallows back the pain. "I could see that your mom was the puppet master, but Meg wanted you, she still does. I know you used to be close. That you went to school together but—"

"She doesn't know how to quit and neither does my mother, that's why I'm quitting them." I trace out her lips with my finger. "I choose you, Laney. If Meg gets stuck in a tree, she's going to have to call the fire department like everybody else. I'll be too busy burying myself in a slice of Heaven."

She gives a soft laugh. "I see what you did there."

"Yeah?" I land a kiss on her lips and moan. "You know who didn't see what I did?"

"The Big N.P.?"

"Precisely." A pale flicker catches my attention out the window. "Look at that."

"It's snowing." She latches onto my arm and gives a squeeze. "It looks like we get a white Christmas after all. You know what they say, if it snows on Christmas, a miracle can happen." Laney gives a sad smile as she looks into my eyes. "I really love you, Ryder Capwell. Thank you for loving me back. I hope you never regret our relationship. I'm sorry what it's costing you."

"The only thing I regret is the year I spent without you. I'm in this forever."

A smile inches up her cheek. "Forever hardly sounds like enough time to be with you."

"You always were the smart one." I give her ribs a little tickle. "Hey why don't you look under the tree? I bet Santa left something there for you a little early."

She inspects the floor surrounding the twirling evergreen and shakes her head. "Looks like Santa forgot. There's nothing under there."

"Why don't you try near the top branch? I bet he tossed it up there. He's always in such a damn hurry."

Laney springs up and hikes to the balls of her feet. "Nope."

I slip the red velvet box out of my pocket and get on bended knee.

"That's because it's down here." I smile up at her sheepishly and crack the box open.

"Ryder!" She cups her hands over her mouth.

"I hope you don't mind." I swallow hard. Laney looks like a princess with the pink and green lights sparkling around her. "I'm actually one year late in giving this to you." I had it worked out for last Christmas, but things didn't exactly go as planned. Having her find me falling into another girl's bed wasn't on the shortlist of how I wanted to propose. "You don't have to answer me, Laney. I know it's only been a few days, and we've just straightened the ship, but I can't help the way I feel. I need you in my life. I'd be more than humbled and honored if you would consider becoming my wife."

Laney falls to her knees with tears running down her face, an ear-to-ear smile that's just for me.

"Ryder." She lands a mouthwatering kiss over my lips that lets me know exactly how she feels. "I do want to answer you." She crashes into me with another quick kiss. "*Yes!* I want to be your wife. I've wanted to marry you for as long as I can remember. I'm not doing this life thing without you."

"Thank you." I touch my palms to her cheeks and kiss her with a tenderness that feels far too restrained for the moment, but I want to savor it, memorize it. "You're the family I choose. This is it—me and you forever."

I take the ring and slip it over her finger. A simple diamond encircled with a series of smaller stones.

"It's beautiful." She holds it out toward the tree and it sparkles like an explosion of miniature shooting stars.

"You're beautiful."

She crushes her lips over mine and lands us to the floor. We indulge in long, lingering kisses that expand beyond the confines of time, right into eternity.

Laney pulls back and gazes at me, content and happy. "We're finally together."

"Looks like we got our Christmas miracle." I wrap my arms around her tight.

"Looks like we did." She gives an impish grin. "You think the Big N.P. can come out to play now?"

"Are you kidding? He's been dying to get out all night. You know what his favorite game is?"

"Seven minutes in Heaven?"

"Yeah, but he cheats. He likes to stay as long as he can."

She pulls me to my feet and leads us to the bedroom. "It's time to get to paradise."

I give a gentle tug to her hand and reel her in.

"Paradise is right here with you."

Our lips find one another as we begin the slow meandering dance to the bedroom. We've got all night, all year—a lifetime.

Paradise was with Laney all along.

And there are no truer words.

Thank you for reading, **Winter Kisses** (3:AM Kisses Book 2). If you enjoyed this novella, please consider leaving a review at your point of purchase.

Sugar Kisses (3:AM Kisses 3) is now available! Look for **Whiskey Kisses** (3:AM Kisses 4) summer 2014. Books 3 and 4 are full length novels.

Acknowledgments

To my readers, thank you for your amazing support. I enjoy all of the friendships we've made, and I love to respond to you through email, facebook, twitter, or my blog. This ride wouldn't be half as fun if it weren't for you.

To all of the bloggers, the betas, the people who I may or may not have cornered to run my ideas by, thank you for all your time and attention. It is much appreciated!

To the awesome Christina Kendler you are a word ninja of the highest order. I salute you! To Rachel Tsoumbakos, who always looks twice, and saves me from many an error, thank you! And finally to the amazing Sarah Freese, how can I ever repay you for your awesomeness? Ready for another book?

Thank you to my kids for doing the dishes. I'm also thankful that each of you has discovered you can do your own laundry and on occasion toss in a few things of mine. I owe you a really nice dinner, your choice. To my husband who still kisses me after all these crazy years. Thank you for that.

To Him who sits on the throne—each day I smile with peace in my heart because I am forgiven. I owe you everything.

About the Author

Addison Moore is a *New York Times*, *USA Today*, and *Wall Street Journal* bestselling author who writes contemporary and paranormal romance. Her work has been featured in *Cosmopolitan* magazine. Previously she worked for nearly a decade as a therapist on a locked psychiatric unit. She resides with her husband, four wonderful children, and two dogs on the West Coast where she eats too much chocolate and stays up way too late. When she's not writing, she's reading.

Please visit her at:
http://addisonmoorewrites.blogspot.com
Facebook: Addison Moore Author
Twitter: @AddisonMoore
Instagram: http://instagram.com/authoraddisonmoore

CPSIA information can be obtained at www.ICGtesting.com
Printed in the USA
LVOW12s1950030216

473521LV00009B/748/P

9 781496 144942